# My Beautiful Hippie

# My Beautiful Hippie

### JANET NICHOLS LYNCH

Holiday House / New York

This is a work of fiction. Names and characters are
the product of the author's imagination. Any resemblance
to actual persons is coincidental.

Library of Congress Cataloging-in-Publication Data

Lynch, Janet Nichols, 1952-
My beautiful hippie / Janet Nichols Lynch. — 1st ed.
p. cm.
Summary: Fifteen-year-old Joanne, raised in San Francisco's Haight District, becomes
involved with Martin, a hippie, and various aspects of the late 1960s cultural revolution
despite her middle-class upbringing.
ISBN 978-0-8234-2603-4 (hardcover)
[1. Coming of age—Fiction.   2. Hippies—Fiction.   3. Family life—California—
Fiction.   4. Pianists—Fiction.   5. Feminism—Fiction.   6. Vietnam War, 1961-1975—
Fiction.   7. San Francisco (Calif.)—History—20th century—Fiction.]
I. Title.
PZ7.L9847My 2013
[Fic]—dc23
2012016563

To my girlfriends
Tina, Marsha, Caryl, Jeffra,
Patricia, and Regina
because you were there
for me then

# CHAPTER
## ONE

I was in a hurry as usual, rushing down the hill on Ashbury Street. Only minutes before Denise's bridal shower was about to start, my mother had sent me to the Sunrise Market for a tub of Cool Whip. I turned the corner on Haight Street and smacked right into him. I looked up into eyes of the palest blue, sparkly with humor, soft with caring. The sun lit up his wavy, honey-brown shoulder-length hair so that its outline appeared like a golden aura. Diagonally across his gauzy shirt was the rainbow strap of the guitar slung on his back.

He was gorgeous, and what did I look like to him? The hem of the turquoise dotted-swiss dress my mother had made hit the middle of my knees, while all around me miniskirts were thigh-high. I wanted to be cool more than anything, but how was that possible with my mother dressing me?

"Spare change?" he asked, palm extended.

"Uh...no." My fingers tightened around two quarters and three pennies, exact change. My mom knew what things cost. My dad had ordered me never to give money to panhandlers. I glanced at the boy's bare feet. If they were clean, he was just some neighborhood kid playing hippie for the weekend, but filthy black and callused meant the real thing. His feet were somewhere in between.

"Sorry," I said.

"Peace." He splayed two fingers in farewell, about to slip away from me.

"I play the guitar," I blurted. I was teaching myself.

"Far out."

"And the piano." It was my life.

"Ah, a kindred spirit! The soul of a musician." His gaze searched my eyes. "You're beautiful." He removed his strand of love beads and placed them over my head.

Next, I was paying for the Cool Whip and didn't even remember walking into the market. Heading back on Haight Street, I nearly stumbled over the bodies that were sitting or lying on the sidewalk. It was 1967, the Summer of Love, and I was fifteen. The Haight District, the San Francisco neighborhood I had grown up in, was crowded with hippies, freaks, heads, beautiful people, flower children—they were called all those things—and the straights who gawked at them from cars and tour buses.

I looked for my beautiful hippie, but he had been swallowed up in the mash of humanity and traffic. Hippies called everyone beautiful, I told myself, but I had already plunged headlong into a deep crush.

Trudging up Ashbury, I tucked the love beads inside the neckline of my dress so my mom wouldn't start asking questions. Two blocks up the hill from commercial Haight Street, I turned left on Frederick, my street, where things were a lot quieter. The hippies tended to swarm over the flatlands: Golden Gate Park to the west, and to the north, Page Street, Oak Street, and the Panhandle, the milelong skinny strip of green jutting out from the park.

I loved our house on its tranquil block. It was a Victorian built in the late 1800s, one of the few that had survived the 1906 San Francisco earthquake and fire. On the left was an octagonal turret with its third-story window, and on the right were two stacked and gabled bay windows. The facade was covered with scalloped shingles, and the whole structure was painted slate gray with white trim. At the street level was a three-foot retaining wall, topped with a wrought-iron fence enclosing our little yard. I scampered up the concrete steps leading to the gate, let myself in, and instead of mounting the sixteen steep stairs leading to the front porch, I took the walkway to the back door. As I entered the kitchen, I pressed my fingers to my love beads through my dress.

"Finally, Joanne!" Mom greeted me. "What took you so long? I had expected some help around here." She was short, with low-slung breasts and a bulging stomach, not particularly fat, but rather a natural product of over forty years of gravitational pull. She was wearing the new pink polyester knit dress she had made and a frilly hostess apron. Her swollen feet oozed out of matching pink high heels and her hair was a lacquered bubble; she had it done every Friday afternoon at the beauty salon.

I set the brown sack of Cool Whip on the counter.

"Not there, Joanne, the refrigerator! Haven't you got any sense?"

I opened the fridge and placed the Cool Whip on top of two other containers of Cool Whip. It was a bad sign. Mom in a panic over Cool Whip. Whenever she entertained, she had to have everything just right, like those pictures of food in *Ladies' Home Journal.*

The doorbell rang, and she dashed out of the kitchen to answer it. She scurried back in, yanked off her apron, and hurried out again.

Jerry Westfield, the groom-to-be, slunk through the back door. "Oh, hi, Beethoven."

"You're not supposed to be here!"

"Hi, Jerry, nice to see you," he said in a falsetto, then hooked an incisor over his lower lip. He was cute, tall and lanky, with big brown eyes and a single, reluctant dimple. My mother referred to him as a "catch." He hovered over the hors d'oeuvres platter and began plucking the pickled herring out of Mom's meticulous arrangement.

"Hey, leave some for somebody else." I grabbed a dish towel, twisted it from the ends, and snapped it at his butt.

"Hey, you! Gimme that!"

I shrieked as he chased me around the table.

Mom returned to the kitchen, her fingertips pressed into her temples. "Heavens, Joanne! Stop that roughhousing."

I pointed at Jerry. "He started it."

"Falsely accused!" He was laughing, the sour cream dressing from the herring wedged in the crease of his mouth.

Mom handed him a tray of manly sandwiches, still bearing crusts, and steered him toward the den, where my dad and my brother, Dan, were already glommed onto the boob tube, watching the Giants game. Mom dabbed fondly at Jerry's mouth and reached up behind him to touch a dark brown curl that had inched over the button-down collar of his white Oxford shirt. "You're going to need a haircut before the wedding. We don't want you looking shaggy in the photographs."

"Sure thing, Helen."

She placed a double-decker bowl of chips and dips in his other hand.

"Where's the beer?" he asked.

The doorbell rang.

"Heavens!" Tiny beads of sweat appeared above Mom's lip. "I'll bring it in, Jerry."

As soon as he left, Mom addressed me in a hushed, frantic tone. "Go see what's keeping your sister. I expected some help around here."

"Oh, Mommy! Everything looks perfect!"

As I mounted the stairs, I heard shrieks of greetings and laughter erupt from the foyer and saw our fat black-and-white cat, Snoopy, scurrying beneath the furniture, back slung low and ears flattened. Denise was in our bedroom, seated at her vanity on the gold swivel stool with the furry pink seat, staring vacantly into the mirror. Only one of the orange juice cans that she used as rollers had been removed, the others still bobby-pinned together in neat rows over her head.

"What are you doing?" I asked. "Mom is down there having a cow."

She offered the single long tendril of released hair. "Feel it. I've been wearing these things twenty-eight hours, and my hair is still damp."

"Bummer." I hated sleeping on rollers, and anyway, my plain

brown hair looked cool long, straight, and parted down the middle. "Can't you hear all those ladies?" I reached for a bobby pin.

"Stop it, Joanne! I'm not going down there with wet hair." Miss Perfect. A few weeks earlier, she had come home crying because she didn't weigh enough to be allowed to join Weight Watchers; she went on Dr. Stillman's Quick-Weight-Loss Diet and nearly floated away on all the water she drank. She used to be smart and witty, a big sister I could look up to, but falling head over heels for Jerry Westfield had turned her into a ninny.

"Is this how you're going to act on your wedding day?" I goaded her. "Are you sure you want to get married so soon?"

"What a question!" She rolled her eyes around our room with the rosebud wallpaper and the frilly pink homemade curtains that matched the frilly pink homemade bedspreads. "I'll be getting out of here." Her voice softened as she looked at me in the mirror with that nauseating glow she'd been wearing through her engagement. "Oh, Joanne, you'll see! When you find the right guy, nothing but him will matter, and everything in your life will slip away."

"Not my piano!"

She emitted a little puff of air. "I didn't expect you to understand."

I got out the hair dryer, released the plastic hood from the nozzle, and blasted hot air over each orange juice can. Denise applied pearly-pink lipstick, rosy-pink blush, blue eye shadow, and thick eyeliner with little check marks at the ends. Together we got all the cans out of her hair. Denise stood, bent over, and brushed her hair forward to add volume. She flipped it back and arranged it in ripples over her shoulders. At last she smiled with self-satisfaction in the vanity mirror.

"Jerry's here," I reported matter-of-factly.

"Gerald's here?" she gasped.

"Uh-huh." If her hair hadn't turned out, I wouldn't have mentioned it. "Maybe he wants to see what presents you get."

"Very funny. He knows this hen party is only for— Oh, my God! Jerry's talking to Mother's *friends* right now?"

"Calm down. He's in the den, watching the Giants game with Dad and Dan."

"That's even worse! Gerald is antiwar and Dan is prowar. Gerald's major is psychology, and Daddy doesn't even believe there's any such thing!"

Denise didn't get it. Jerry was eventually going to find out all about us unsophisticated Donnellys. It was only a matter of time. "Your bridal shower has been going on without you for a half hour."

"I need to compose myself," she said wearily. "Tell Mother I'll be right down."

As I passed Mom's sewing room, I noticed Denise's massive white wedding gown and four pink empire-waist bridesmaid's dresses hanging at attention across the closet. Of course my mother had made them all. If she staged an event and it didn't knock her off her feet for three days afterward, then she hadn't put enough effort into it. After Denise's wedding, Mom would have to go to a rest home or the nuthouse in Napa.

Downstairs, Mom was relating her latest favorite story in her loud bray to a circle of her dearest, oldest friends whom she rarely saw. "He was her psychology *professor*! On the first day of class he looked out in that auditorium of three hundred brand-new freshmen, laid eyes on our Denise, and just *had* to have her!"

"Isn't he still a graduate student?" asked Maxine Fulmer. She had gained quite a bit of weight since her husband had left her for his much younger secretary last year. She wore an African-print kaftan, big jewelry, and no bra, her breasts basking on her front like seal pups.

Mom's mouth hung slightly open, as if holding her place in her story. "Jerry is getting his PhD, and soon he'll be a psychoanalyst!"

"He's a Freudian?" Mrs. Fulmer flopped back on the sofa cushions and slapped her lap. "God help your poor child, Helen."

"Denise will be right down," I announced.

Mom drew me near and whispered, "Pass the hors d'oeuvres trays, Joanne." She made her way to another group of friends and said, "He was her psychology *professor*! On the first day of class he looked out in that auditorium of three hundred brand-new freshmen, laid eyes on our Denise, and just *had* to have her!"

I rushed over to my best friend, Rena, the one person I had been allowed to invite. Her eyes were done up like Twiggy's, false eyelashes and two colors of shadow, and her lipstick was Yardley's pearl white. Her black, waist-length hair was in snarls because it took so long to comb out. We greeted each other with squeals, waving two peace signs at each other and leaping around in circles. Nobody understood me like Rena.

I glanced over my shoulder to be sure my mother wasn't looking, then flashed Rena my love beads. "I met someone," I whispered.

"Where? When? Who *is* he?"

"I'll tell you later. Let's go get the hors d'oeuvres before my mom has kittens."

As we passed Mom, she called, "I see you've recruited some help, Joanne. Thank you, Serena."

Rena cringed when she heard her hated complete name. After years of tremendous effort, she had succeeded in getting most people to call her Rena, but my mother had known her since we were in the third grade, and to her, Rena would always be Serena. It only proved that to become the person you wanted to be, you had to move far, far away from everyone who had watched you grow up.

Our kitchen was yellow with barnyard wallpaper. My mom was wild about roosters. They were on our plates, towels, and appliance cozies. Rena eyed the large white sheet cake, which read CONGRATULATIONS ON YOUR WEDDING, DENISE, THE FIRST DAY OF THE REST OF YOUR LIFE.

Rena looked at me knowingly and whispered, "The first day of the *end* of her life."

We howled with laughter. Rena and I had big plans. After college, we were going to live together in New York City, where she would act on Broadway and I would attend Juilliard and play recitals at Carnegie Hall.

By the time we returned to the living room with the hors d'oeuvres trays, Denise had made her entrance.

"Where will you live?" asked our cousin, Beth, one of the bridesmaids.

"In an apartment near campus. A darling place on Shattuck."

"What's your major?" asked Judy, one of Denise's neighborhood friends.

"Art history, but...well..." Denise gave a brave smile. "I won't be returning to classes in the fall." Usually the docile, obedient daughter, Denise had fought Mom tooth and nail to allow her to cross the Bay Bridge every day, alone, by bus to attend the University of California in Berkeley instead of going to local San Francisco State College. Now she was giving it all up after one year to marry Jerry.

"Why would she continue?" asked Thelma Newman, my mother's best friend. She was a small woman and, like my mom, wore a polyester double-knit dress and kept her hair in a lacquered bubble. "She's getting her M.R.S. That's really the only reason a girl needs to go to a university."

"It isn't *that,*" said Denise, flustered. "Gerald's stipend just isn't enough for us to live on. I'll be working as a secretary here in the city, on Market, while he finishes his doctorate. Then we'll be set."

"What if you get pregnant?" asked Beth.

Denise blushed beneath her blusher as if all the ladies were imagining her doing what it took to get pregnant. "Oh, we aren't planning to start a family for several years."

"Thank God for the Pill," said Judy.

"Oh, Denise would never take such a thing!" said Mom, but I knew Denise already was taking it, having timed it precisely so that its effectiveness would kick in on her wedding night.

"You're getting a prenuptial agreement, I hope," said Mrs. Fulmer.

Denise cleared her throat and said in a whiny, indignant tone, "Oh, I don't believe that's necessary."

"No blushing bride ever did," said Mrs. Fulmer. "Until now. Times are changing, Denise. Women are demanding their rights. Suppose you work for several years, your husband finishes his doctorate, sets up a thriving practice, and then dumps you for the prettiest patient with the biggest emotional problems. At least you would be assured of financial compensation, an opportunity to complete your education." Recently Mrs. Fulmer had shocked all her friends by returning to the university herself to complete the degree she had started over twenty years ago. She wagged her finger at Denise. "I'd look into it if I were you, dear, for peace of mind."

The awkward silence in the room was pierced by Denise's silvery laugh. "I trust Gerald implicitly."

"Look at that mound of presents, Denise! " exclaimed Mom, clapping her hands together. "Hadn't you better get started?" She handed me the telephone notepad and a pen. "Joanne, you be recording secretary for Denise's thank-you notes." She handed Rena a paper plate with slits cut into it. "Here, Serena, you make the ribbon bouquet for the wedding rehearsal. Slip the ends in like so, the bows on top."

Denise unwrapped an olive-green fondue pot. Then an orange one. After the fourth fondue pot, she glanced across the room at Mom's worried face. The two of them had fought over Denise's choice of silver pattern, and the fact that she hadn't gotten a single dessert fork only proved that Mom had been right in warning her against registering something so expensive.

A male voice erupted from the den. "Honey? Honey?"

The women's conversation died down.

"Honey, could you get us some beers?" called Jerry.

Mom's palms flew to her cheeks. "Those poor men! I completely forgot about their beer."

Mrs. Newman patted Denise's knee. "Hop to it, dear. You want him to keep thinking he's one lucky fellow."

"Hmph," said Mrs. Fulmer, crossing her arms over her unrestrained bosom, her eyes following Denise's progress out of the room.

After the cake was cut, Rena and I escaped with our pieces into the privacy of the bedroom, which would soon be all mine.

"Out with it," said Rena. "Tell me every juicy detail."

I tried to make my encounter with the beautiful hippie as

thrilling as possible, but at the end of my story, Rena merely raised one side of her upper lip. "That's it? He asked for spare change and gave you love beads? You don't know a thing about him."

"His eyes, Rena. He has dreamy eyes. He plays guitar! And you shoulda seen the cool way his jeans sorta hung off his hipbones."

"How old?"

"Dunno. Seventeen, eighteen." I gulped. "Maybe older."

"Too old for you. Long hair?"

I tapped my shoulders with my fingertips. "Groovy."

Rena rolled her eyes. "We weren't gonna do this ever again. 'Member? No teenybopper crushes. We aren't gonna fall for a guy just cuz he's cute. We're gonna get to know him first. He's gonna call all the time, take us out on dates, then maybe, just maybe we might get interested."

I winced. "I thought that just meant for the boys at school."

"Nope. *All* boys."

"You're right," I said grudgingly. "I spent so many lunch periods hanging around playing guitars with Dave. Then he goes and asks me for Terry Schumacher's number."

"Terry Schumacher is a nothing," said Rena. Terry had actually been sophomore homecoming princess. Rena and I had a better chance of being the first women on the moon than of being homecoming princesses.

"Sure, Terry's cute and sweet," said Rena, "but she hardly ever says a word."

"Guys don't like smart girls."

"Or ones with opinions. 'Member when Rusty asked me to the movies? He goes, 'What do ya want to see?' and I go, '*The Graduate, Cool Hand Luke*, or *Guess Who's Coming to Dinner*. You pick from those.' After that one date, when I asked him why he was ignoring me, he goes, 'When I ask a girl what she wants to see, I expect her to say whatever I want to see.'"

I had never been asked on a date, just kissed once at music camp. It was a slimy, teeth-knocking kiss, and I had hid from the boy the rest of camp, afraid he would try it again, even though I had liked him before the kiss.

Rena was rummaging through her huge suede bag bordered with long fringe. She withdrew a 45 RPM record, exclaiming, "Hey! Look what I scored!" It was "Evolution! Revolution!" by a new San Francisco group, the Purple Cockroach, which was quickly becoming known simply as Roach. The hit single had soared up the Bay Area chart past the Jefferson Airplane's "Somebody to Love" and the Doors' "Light my Fire," and had been number one for three weeks.

"Far out!" I exclaimed, lifting the lid of my record player.

On the record's paper sleeve were four hairy guys sitting in a tree, glaring vacantly into the camera. Rena pointed to the guy front and center, who had a white man's light brown Afro, a wiry black beard, and penetrating eyes. "Gus Abbott is so out of sight."

I put the record on the turntable and placed the needle on it, and a blast of psychedelic rock erupted: loud drums, warbling reverb, and shouts of "Evolution! Revolution! We gotta be free, free, free! Break those chains of society!"

Rena and I bobbed our heads and shook our bodies until Mom shouted up the stairs, "Turn that racket down!"

"I saw some auditions posted for this play the Buena Vista Players are putting on," said Rena. "Will you come with me?"

"To the Buena Vista? I guess." The previous month, the theater had been shut down on an obscenity charge because it staged a reading of Michael McClure's *The Beard*. "What's the play?"

"It's called *The Blacks*. I don't know anything about it."

"Are you worried about foul language?"

"My mom won't care." Rena was kind of a rebel, and her mom backed her up. In junior high, when she was suspended three times for wearing slacks to school, Mrs. Thompson insisted they were more modest than miniskirts and warmer. In our freshman year the principal gave in and let girls wear pants to school.

The record ended, and I shifted the arm of the phonograph to the edge to play it again.

"What's this?" Rena picked up a newspaper clipping propped on my desk:

### Hitchhiker Check Is
### Revealing

The California Highway Patrol checked out 100 hitchhikers over a three-month period on a stretch of Highway 101. Consider this: exactly 84 had criminal records. And 12 either were runaways or servicemen absent without official leave. That left four, just four, who hadn't been crossways with the law, or were about to be.

"My mom—she's always using scare tactics to try to get me to behave. She and Dad never worried about Denise doing anything wrong, and they let Dan do stuff cuz he's a boy."

"Does Jerry know Denise is super-smart? She seems too young to get married."

"I know, but Jerry's *old*—twenty-three. She probably just wants to give it up and be done with it."

"You mean, like, her *virginity*?" Rena squealed, rolling her eyes. "We're living in a sexual revolution!"

"Not Denise. I hear her fighting Jerry off downstairs late at night, when they come in from dates. Jerry lives with his aunt in Orinda, and they have no place to go to be alone together."

"Bummer. Well, at least as a married lady she can use tampons."

We both hated those big old smelly sanitary napkins, which hooked on the metal stays of an elastic belt and felt like wearing a diaper.

I looked straight into Rena's Twiggy eyes. "Will you help me find him?"

She knew I meant my beautiful hippie. "Where will we look?"

"Around. He's probably roaming the street right now." I gazed up at the wall hanging I had sewn with yarn on burlap: music notes, a turquoise guitar, and the saying, "Out of my loneliness I will fashion a song, and when I find someone who understands, we will sing it together." I looked back at Rena and said, "He's perfect for me."

"How could he be perfect if your dad won't let him in the house?"

That evening after the shower guests left and Jerry and Denise slipped away for a dinner date, my parents, Mrs. Newman, Dan, and I sat among the ruins of the party and scarfed leftovers. Ladies' party food—clam-stuffed marinated mushrooms, surprise meatballs (raspberry preserves was the surprise), curried deviled eggs, rolled watercress and blue cheese sandwiches, and the floating islands of melted rainbow sherbet in the bride's punch—was a rare treat for Dad and Dan, but I was stuffed from eating all afternoon.

"Pass me the deviled eggs, Dick," Mom said.

"Sure, sure," said Dad. I wondered why anyone named Richard would want to go by Dick. Didn't Dad know what it meant? It embarrassed me every time my mom used it.

I gazed forlornly at my upright piano in the corner of the room, my Beethoven sonata open on the music rack. I usually practiced at least two hours a day, but with all the frantic preparations for the shower, I hadn't gotten around to it yet and craved the feel of the smooth keys.

Snoopy emerged from his hiding place and rubbed against our legs, purring loudly, and when Dad wasn't looking, I fed him bits of clam stuffing. I leafed through the July 7 issue of *Time* magazine, as if I were not the least bit interested in the cover story "The Hippies: Philosophy of a Subculture," which I would pore over in private, hoping to glean something I didn't already know. The words "Haight-Ashbury" seemed to fly off the page. Amazing! Our little neighborhood—the hub of a cultural revolution!

It was warm, and all the windows were open. A trolley rumbled by and made a wide, sweeping turn up the block onto Masonic Avenue. Next, the Gray Line Tour bus roared past, farting nauseous diesel fumes on its Hippie Hop, advertised as "a safari through psychedelphia, and the only foreign tour within the continental limits of the United States." Apparently the hippies had blocked off traffic on Haight Street, with their chants of "The streets belong to the people," "We are free," and "Haight is love." An overflow of pedestrians roamed our street, and strains of songs, conversation, laughter, flutes, bells, tambourines, and drums wafted into our living room. Hippies had begun moving into the Haight in 1965, and it looked like the party was only getting started. I loved all the excitement, but my parents were fed up and threatened to move.

Looking over the sofa back, out the bay window, my dad scowled at a long-haired couple ambling by arm in arm. "You can't tell the girl from the boy."

"Hippies are a social disease," scoffed Dan, the only boy in the Haight sporting a crew cut. In the news, the city's health director, Ellis D. ("LSD") Sox, had warned that there was a danger in the Haight of epidemic hepatitis, venereal disease, typhus, and malnutrition, but after inspecting dozens of hippie pads and establishments, the health department hadn't found anything wrong. "Hippies are always looking for a free handout," continued Dan. "They should get a job."

"*You* should get a job," I retorted.

Dad slapped his knee. He had a paunch and a bald dome, with a ring of black-and-gray hair curling around it. He was a sales rep for a produce company and made his calls to the grocery stores of the city dressed in a business suit. "You fell right into that one, son."

Dan scowled at me. "I'm looking for work. I'm not a hippie hypocrite."

"Meaning what?" I asked.

"Hippies say 'make love, not war,' but that's just an excuse to have sex all the time."

Mom held her palms to her ears, shuddering at the word "sex." "Kids, stop your bickering!"

"They're anti-American," said Dan. "Can't appreciate what the boys are doing in Vietnam for them. Just wait until they live in a Communist state. Let's see how free they are."

Dan leaped from the sofa in agitation, dropped to the floor, and began pumping out push-ups. He had recently graduated from high school, where he had been active in JROTC—Junior Reserve Officer Training Corps. He couldn't wait to join the marines and hop over to Nam to take potshots at "Charlie," but our parents were making him attend City College for two years first. With a student deferment, he had to be satisfied with living the war vicariously through letters from his buddy Jimmy Howe, who was marching through faraway rice paddies to blast away Commie gooks.

"Freedom isn't free," agreed Dad, who had enlisted in the navy after the bombing of Pearl Harbor, knowing he would be drafted.

"I'll be ready," said Dan, grunting. "When I test for the marines, I'm going to score the highest in fitness."

"You have to take a written test, too," I reminded him.

"I can *read*." It was true Dan was smart enough. He got Cs and Ds in school only because he didn't try.

He disgusted me—his veins popping out of his arms and neck, the sweat dampening his hair, and the stench of his BO wafting through the room.

He and I had never gotten along. Growing up, he rarely let me join in his play, but if I was doing something with my friends he wanted to do, he'd bust his way in. During board games, he'd cheat and throw the game pieces if he wasn't winning; I taunted him with "Devil Dan! Devil Dan!" The last couple of years we'd hardly spoken to each other.

"That Maxine Fulmer has gone off the deep end," said my mother, eager to change the subject.

"She fancies herself a *feminist*." Mrs. Newman pronounced the word as if she had bitten into something rotten.

"It's a shame," said Mom. "She's not an unattractive woman, even with all that weight she's gained."

"Oh, Maxine was simply stunning before she let herself go," said Mrs. Newman, "and stopped wearing a bra."

That was it for the guys. Dad and Dan both slunk out of the room. We women started in on the cleanup. When I thought I had done my share, I attempted to slip out the back door.

"Hold it, Joanne. You've got no business out on the street this late," said Mom.

"It's only seven-thirty. I'm just going down to the store for some gum."

"You don't need it."

"Mom, please! I'll be right back."

She hesitated, but I could tell I was going to win this argument. She and Mrs. Newman were dying to have a heart-to-heart without "talking in a cornfield" with my big ears around. "You have money for gum?"

I pulled a rumpled dollar bill out of my pocket that I had earned by babysitting.

"You break that dollar now and the whole thing will be gone within the week."

"Here, Joanne, I have a nickel for you." Mrs. Newman removed her coin purse from her handbag.

"Gee, thanks."

"That is completely unnecessary, Thelma," said Mother. "Don't let me forget to pay you back."

"You're not paying me back, Helen. I won't hear of it."

I made my escape. Even with Mrs. Newman's nickel, I was breaking that dollar. If I ever got another chance to give spare change to my beautiful hippie, I was going to take it.

# CHAPTER TWO

I looked and looked for him, in the Good Karma Coffeehouse, in the Psychedelic Store, on Hippie Hill, and all along Haight Street. Could he have been a runaway just passing through? He didn't have a backpack, and he didn't look hungry, filthy, or scared. He didn't even look like he needed the money he was panhandling. Maybe he was just another middle-class kid living with his family like me, but where was he?

On Wednesday evening, I walked a block down Ashbury and turned on Rena's street, Walker. We continued down the hill one more block to Haight, then headed toward the Buena Vista Community Theater.

Rena was wearing a purple paisley minidress with a skirt that rode up nearly to her underpants. My parents would never have let me out of the house dressed like that, but Rena's parents were so busy trying to break up, they never bothered her. They'd nearly succeeded in divorcing five years ago, but had had Rena's little brother, Markie, instead.

Rena pointed up the street. "Hey, there's Lisa and Candy!"

I frowned. "Let's pretend we don't even know them." During freshman and sophomore years Rena and I had struggled for a position on the fringe of the in crowd. I did Lisa Girardi's homework and gave Candy Lambert the homemade chocolate chip cookies out of my lunch, but that was over. I was done with that snotty bunch now, even if Rena wasn't.

Rena bit her lip, and her brow creased. "What happened at Kent's wasn't Lisa's fault."

"I don't care! I hate them all! They're not our friends, and they never will be!" All last year, Lisa's boyfriend, Kent Dougal, had called me "skag." On the last day of school, he threw a bash because his parents were out of town. It was one of those friends-asking-friends-of-friends affairs, with a garage band playing "Louie, Louie" and "Gloria" and a few other three-chord hits. Kent got on the microphone and announced, "This is a private party, and Joanne Donnelly, you weren't invited." How could I ever live down such humiliation?

Lisa and Candy went into Love Burgers, and I was glad to avoid them.

"I hope we're not the first ones at the audition," said Rena.

"We could walk slower."

Rena hugged herself and pouted. "I don't know why I'm wasting my time. I probably won't get a part."

"Sure you will."

"Probably won't even get call backs."

"You will."

In front of the Drogstore Cafe, Rena sniffed. As usual, the smell of pot permeated the air. We inhaled deeply and held our breath until we burst out laughing.

"I don't believe there really is such a thing as a contact high," said Rena. "We'd be stoned all the time."

"Yeah." I didn't know what being stoned felt like, but I was pretty sure it hadn't happened to me.

"We gotta get some grass," said Rena.

"Yeah, but where?"

"Oh, I can't imagine," said Rena, and we laughed again. Pot was everywhere in the Haight, and cheap, too, but neither of us had the nerve to buy it because we knew that undercover cops, or "narcs," sometimes pretended to sell it. We wouldn't dare "hold" because if our parents found it, they'd ground us for life.

My mom had read somewhere that marijuana was a "gateway" drug. She warned me that if I took a single puff, I'd be a heroin addict for life.

"Oh, well," I said. "Someday someone will offer us a hit, and we'll take it."

"Yeah, and we'll drop acid, too."

"Oh, I don't know, Rena."

"Don't you want to have the ultimate psychedelic experience?"

"LSD is scary." I'd seen a young runaway freaking out on a bad trip in front of the Free Clinic, having not quite made it to the Calm Room inside. She was screaming and writhing on the sidewalk as people held her down, trying to prevent her from ripping out her eyes.

I nearly knocked into a guy in an American flag top hat and pink tutu, juggling bananas. He tossed a banana at Rena and she caught it.

"Which end do you light?" I asked, and we laughed. There was a rumor that smoking dried banana peels had hallucinogenic effects; it was even in Donovan's song "Mellow Yellow."

Rena peeled the banana and offered it to me. I took a big bite.

We hiked up the steep path through the dense foliage of Buena Vista Park, which indeed had a "good view" overlooking the city and bay. By the time we entered the theater, we were both breathless from the climb.

The houselights were down, and two adult Negroes were on the lit stage, holding scripts and yelling gross language that embarrassed me. There were about fifty people sitting in the first three rows of the theater. Rena nudged me with her hip to take a seat toward the middle.

The actors finished their reading and the director, a paunchy white guy, looked at his clipboard and called out two names. Two other Negroes came up and began to read the same scene.

Rena whispered, "I'm not on the list, Jo."

I whispered back, "Go put your name in."

"Naw, I'll just wait till a break."

Several people turned around and gave us stern looks for talking. The director called out two more names, and two Negro women took the stage to spew obscenities at each other. I stared at the silhouettes of the people seated before us, a row of round Afros, like the heads of dandelions, and a realization slowly crept over the back of my head.

When the female readers finished, I grabbed Rena's hand. "We're leaving," I whispered. I got up and yanked her out of her seat.

"Are you crazy? I want to audition!"

"No, you don't," I said emphatically into her face. As I tried to pull her along, she planted her feet and stuck out her butt. Our commotion attracted the attention of some of the people, who began to laugh and mutter among themselves.

The director half-called, half-chuckled, "Can I help you girls?"

"No!" I shouted back. "We were just watching." With one mighty pull, I dragged Rena through the foyer and out the door. I ran down the steep hill, through the park, Rena following.

"Dammit it, Jo. What's wrong?" she asked breathlessly. "Is it the cussing?"

"What did you say the play was?"

"*The Blacks*."

"That's what wrong."

Rena stopped, stared at me a moment, then flung her hands to her face. "Oh, my God! I'm ruined!"

I released a strangled laugh that sounded more like a yelp.

"Joanne! How will I ever be able to go to another audition in this city? Every time I show up they'll be pointing at me and saying, 'There's the white girl who tried out for '*The Blacks*.'" She pointed ahead of her for emphasis.

I followed her finger to three guys walking down Haight Street. "There he is!" I exclaimed.

Rena didn't have to ask who. She squinted in the dusk. "Which one?"

"The middle one." This time my beautiful hippie was not wearing a guitar, but an Edwardian top hat, the wind gently lifting his hair beneath it. I fingered the love beads I had worn since the day he had given them to me. When I was at home, around my family, I kept them hidden under my clothes, but when I was out on the street, I displayed them. It was hard to remember to keep adjusting them, and once, Denise had caught me with them. She had questioned me sternly, and I'd lied, saying Rena had made them for me. Apparently Denise hadn't mentioned them to Mom or I'd have been in trouble.

"Let's go talk to him," Rena said.

I quickened my step. "What will we say?"

"Something hip!"

"Something cool!"

We broke into a run. The tramping of our feet and our shrieks of laughter caused him to turn. I grabbed a wad of the loose material on Rena's shoulder and yanked her around the corner of the Drogstore Cafe. "Why do we have to hide?" she whispered.

"I don't know!" We were anything but cool. Just trying to be cool made it impossible to be cool.

I peered through the side and front windows of the Drogstore, over the rows of antique apothecary jars. My hippie and his two companions were waiting at the trolley stop. "What if they get on?" I asked.

"Then we get on," said Rena.

"We're either on the bus or off the bus," we recited together.

When the trolley arrived, the three guys settled in seats toward the front, while we scurried past them and sat toward the back. As we rambled through the city, the three guys talked loudly to one another and shifted in their seats. Whenever my hippie turned to look at the guy behind him, we ducked. I didn't know why.

Rena began, "The guy with the beard, sitting next to your guy—"

"Shhh!" My face burned at the expression "your guy." I was acting like a silly teenybopper, but I couldn't help it.

"—looks like Gus Abbott of Roach."

"Get real! A rock star riding the streetcar? He'd have a limo."

The trolley made stops throughout the North Beach: first on Washington Square near all the coffee shops and Italian restaurants, then on diagonal Columbus Street, notorious for its topless clubs and the improvisational theater troupe the Committee, then near touristy Fisherman's Wharf. On Beach Street, a few blocks west of Ghirardelli Square and the Cannery, one of the guys reached up and pulled the cable to request a stop. They stood to get off the trolley, but my hippie abruptly turned and walked down the aisle of the car to exit through the back door.

As he passed us, he flashed a peace sign and his beautiful smile. His eyes looked into mine, and I thought I detected a spark of recognition, which sent shivers through my body.

The guys crossed the street, entered an opened gate, and climbed a steep walkway leading to a large, shabby Victorian.

Now I was pretty sure I knew where he lived. I sighed deeply. Rena giggled.

# CHAPTER
# THREE

Practicing Beethoven's "*Pathétique*" sonata, I bogged down in the long, difficult development section of the first movement. I had started practicing at two o'clock, needed to go to four, but it was only three-twenty. I was bored, restless, wanted to be done. I leaned back so I could look out the bay window. I wanted to be outside searching for *him*. I sighed, stared back at my music. If I truly wanted to be a concert pianist, I had to sit there, suffering and struggling through.

Since the second grade, I had taken piano lessons from Mrs. Scudder, who lived in the neighborhood, on Cole Street. She was sweet and encouraging and never lost patience. When I passed a piece, Mrs. Scudder allowed me to select a sticker from her sticker tray, lick it, and attach it to my music. When I learned ten pieces by heart, she gave me a four-inch bust of a composer, and after nine years, a couple dozen of them were crowded on a shelf in my bedroom.

Last year Mrs. Scudder hadn't had much to say during my lessons. It didn't seem like I was getting any better, nothing close to Suyu Li, a neighborhood girl a year older than me. At our school's spring talent show, Suyu had whipped through Chopin's Revolutionary Etude with such tremendous speed, accuracy, and passion that the audience members had risen to their feet with thunderous applause. Burning with envy, I asked Suyu afterward how she got so good. She told me it was because of her teacher, Dr. William Harold. She said I would have to audition for him, but she thought I was good enough to get into his studio.

First I had to convince my mother I needed a new piano teacher. Dr. Harold, I found out, charged twice as much as Mrs. Scudder; I would have to attend both a private lesson and a master class with his other students every week, and his studio was in Pacific Heights, two streetcar transfers away. At first my mother gave me a flat-out no. I begged and pleaded with her. I told her I would pay half of my lesson fees from my babysitting money. "What about Mrs. Scudder's feelings?" she asked me. "You would have to tell her you want to quit taking lessons."

I did tell her, at my last lesson of the school year. "I'm so surprised to hear this, Joanne," Mrs. Scudder said. "I thought you loved the piano." I had to look away from her slackened face as she pressed into my hand a statuette I hadn't earned, of a composer I'd never heard of. "I've never had a student make it all the way up to Smetana," she said.

When I auditioned for Dr. Harold, he didn't have much to say about my playing except "Uh-huh, uh-huh." He asked me if I had ever played Beethoven's *"Pathétique,"* and when I said I hadn't, I vowed to learn it by heart over the summer and have it ready to play for him at my first lesson in September. Then I got a disappointing letter stating that I wasn't accepted into his studio, but placed on a waiting list as a "promising candidate."

"I'm sure Mrs. Scudder will take you back," said Mom.

I wasn't going back. Stoically I practiced on my own for the whole month of June with no prospect of a teacher, until I got a postcard from Dr. Harold, sent from the Aspen Summer Music Festival, where he was teaching and performing, which announced an opening for me in his studio. This was the motivation I needed to work even harder on my Beethoven, but now, on this lazy July afternoon, here I sat with forty more minutes to practice.

I flipped backward in the music and thumped through the solemn opening minor chords, making them all *forte*, when I knew some were soft. On the next page I sped up on the runs, knowing I should keep a steady tempo but enjoying how flashy I sounded. I imagined myself under a spotlight in Carnegie Hall, with the marquee outside reading PIANIST JOANNE DONNELLY TONIGHT! SOLD OUT!

I glossed over the fingerings I hadn't quite worked out. Dr. Harold wouldn't expect me to be perfect my first lesson. I needed to leave him something to teach me. When I reached the end of the movement, the clock on the mantel read 3:44. I could stand it no longer. I leaped from the piano bench and made a dash for the back door, nearly tripping over the sixty-foot phone cord Mom had installed so she could do her housework while clutching the receiver between her shoulder and ear, delivering to Mrs. Newman up-to-the-minute reports on the progress of her latest sewing project and dinner preparations.

Mom held the receiver to her bosom to ask, "Done already?"

"I practiced two hours! I need to get out of here."

Without waiting for her reply, I dashed toward Masonic Avenue and didn't stop until I reached Haight Street. I stepped around a guy in a white robe who was painting daisies on the sidewalk in yellow and green Day-Glo paint. He reached out and dotted the top of my shoe with a single petal. I let out a yelp and bunny-hopped away.

I saw a crowd spilling onto the sidewalk in front of the Tangerine Kangaroo. It had the cheapest coffee, used books and magazines to read, chessboards, sewing kits, a piano, a saggy sofa, and a stage. Anyone who wanted to got up and performed as the muse struck them. I stood on tiptoe and peeked through the heads of the crowd, and there was my beautiful hippie onstage, strumming his guitar and crooning Bob Dylan's "The Times They Are A-Changin.'" His voice was much smoother than Dylan's, yet raspy in places for emotional effect. Between verses he improvised a guitar interlude that was not on Dylan's recording. I loved to hop around and flail my arms to the hard, pounding screech of the acid rockers on the San Francisco scene—Janis Joplin, the Jefferson Airplane, the Doors, the Purple Cockroach, the Grateful Dead—but closer to my heart were the folkies: Dylan, Arlo

Guthrie, Joan Baez, Joni Mitchell, Peter, Paul and Mary, Judy Collins, Phil Ochs, and my favorites, Simon and Garfunkel, with their flowing melodies, soulful lyrics, and soothing acoustic guitars. Folk rock was something I could do: sit on my bed, strum a few chords, and sing a simple tune.

When my hippie finished the song, he stood, took a bow, and set his guitar down to indicate he was done with his set. People approached him and rained change into his open guitar case. I waited for them to clear before I made my way toward him. I was wearing a homemade outfit of bell-bottom jeans and a flowered cotton blouse with a Peter Pan collar, the top two buttons unfastened to reveal the love beads he'd given me. My heart was hammering and sweat dampened the quarter I clutched in my hand as I tried to think of something to say to him.

Only a skinny hippie girl with a headband of feathers and a skimpy halter dress was still talking to him. She was smiling and staring intently into his eyes, and he was smiling and staring back. Was she his girlfriend? No, she didn't talk like a girlfriend. She was like me, trying to find an excuse to get to know him, her easy chatter peppered with "far out," "groovy," and "beautiful." She had something commercials on the boob tube called sex appeal. In my dorky homemade clothes, I felt I was no match for her. At last the girl sauntered away, and he turned to me.

I tossed my quarter into his guitar case. "I really liked your song."

"Thanks."

"You play really good."

"Yeah?" His pale blue eyes sparkled.

"And sing. You sing better than Dylan."

He laughed. "Everyone sings better than Dylan."

"I play guitar."

"I know. You told me."

"You remember me?" I nearly shouted in surprise. I wished I could be cool.

"I gave you those beads. It's very important to give, you know? Feeds the soul. But it hurts some people, you know? That's why I panhandle—not to get, but to give folks an opportunity to give. Uptight straights visiting the Haight. They get a real pinched expression on their faces when they hand over their quarters."

I felt a hot blush rise up from my Peter Pan collar. "I'm not a visitor! I live here. I didn't have any extra money that day and—"

He waved a lazy palm to stop me. "It's cool."

I had failed miserably at impressing this beautiful boy, who assumed he had me all figured out when he didn't know me at all. Rena had warned me; I should've listened. All my hoping and fantasizing had come to nothing. A hot indignation bloomed in my throat, and my eyes welled up. I swung around to rush out of the place, but his hand caught my elbow, slid down my arm, and clasped my hand.

"Hey, now."

"My mother sent me to the store with exact change and—" My chin trembled and I looked down in utter humiliation.

"You sure cry easy. Are you a sad person?"

When I shook my head, my tears sprinkled him a little. "No, I'm a happy person," I said to the floor. "I just *feel* things hard. I used to think everybody did, that all people feel alike."

"Not everybody."

"I *am* giving."

"I wasn't talking about you. Those straights that—"

"Look like me?"

"Ah, hell."

When he took me in his arms, I thought, This is it. This is just where I want to be. He held me and rocked me a good long minute or so, and when he let go, he handed me the yellow bandana he'd been using as a headband. Blotting my tears, I inhaled his smell: sandalwood, patchouli, essence of weed.

Out of his guitar case, he pocketed a few dollar bills, then scooped up the rest of the money, walked across the room, and deposited it in the pickle jar set on the counter, marked DIGGER FUND.

He packed up his guitar, and we walked out of the Tangerine Kangaroo together.

Out on the sidewalk, he hesitated. "We should get together sometime."

"Where?" I asked, too eagerly. Not cool.

"Could you come to my pad?"

"Where do you live?" I asked.

"North Beach. Didn't you see what house I turned into that night you and your friend were on the same trolley?"

I attempted a wide-eyed innocent look. "I was on the same streetcar as you? When?" Some of the things Rena and I did were just too embarrassing to admit to.

He grinned. "It's 614 Beach Street."

"When?"

He shrugged. "Whenever. If you come around dinnertime, I'll fix you a meal."

"What day?"

"Like, any day. All days are good, right?"

How could I just drop by his house without him expecting me? I wanted to ask for his phone number but heard my mother's voice echoing in my head: You can't get a boy by chasing him. "Okay, cool. Anytime, then. Oh! What's your name?"

"Martin."

"Joanne."

"See you around."

We flashed peace signs in farewell, then parted ways, him toward the Panhandle for the free Digger meal and me toward home for my mom's Shake 'n Bake chicken and Rice-A-Roni, the San Francisco treat.

"Oh, can I have my bandana back?" he called after me.

I turned to face him, walking backward, smiling broadly, nearly delirious with joy. "Nope. It's important to give, you know. Feeds the soul."

He laughed. He was so beautiful, the ends of his hair alight in the sun.

# CHAPTER FOUR

The wedding was held at All Saints' Episcopal Church on Walker Street, where we had attended services sporadically, maybe six or seven Sundays in a row, then had lost interest for a few months or years before returning for another few Sundays. When I was little, I went to Sunday school there for a while, but all I remembered about it was that once I filled a shoe box lid with plaster of Paris, then stuck a plastic Jesus into it and some shells around him. I don't know why.

Our pastor, Father Leon Harris, had donated some office space in the church basement for the Diggers, a hippie organization that provided a runaway location service, counseling, food, shelter, and medical assistance to street people. When parishioners complained, Father Harris said God's church was meant to help the needy, but the parishioners argued that the kids wouldn't be needy if they had stayed at home with their middle-class families.

Looking over the guests on the bride's side, I saw relatives, neighbors including Rena and her parents, family friends, and a bunch of people I didn't know, probably Dad's business associates. I also spotted Lisa Girardi and Candy Lambert. What were *they* doing here? Then I remembered that Lisa's dad owned a grocery store up on Divisadero Street, and she'd probably invited Candy. I was having a great summer and had been able to forget the misery that the popular kids put me through at school. I hoped their presence wouldn't wreck my day.

The groom's side was far less populated. Jerry was an only child, and his parents were conservative Southern California types from Orange County. Denise had wept over the fact that Mr. and Mrs. Westfield were not in favor of the marriage in general or Denise specifically, an unclear point. The Westfields had been paying for Jerry's education, but Mr. Westfield insisted that a married man stood on his own two feet, and they were therefore cutting off further support. When they met our family at the rehearsal dinner, they were polite but cool toward my parents. Mr. Westfield, who had made a killing in the real estate business, smoked a pipe and stared off in the distance as if we bored him out of his gourd. Mrs. Westfield, a little toothpick of a woman who wore short skirts and draped herself with fox furs with the heads and paws still attached, looked Denise up and down a lot. I'm not sure if they thought they were better than us, but Mom was convinced that they were.

Jerry had not gotten that haircut he'd promised my mom, *and* he wore love beads over his powder-blue dinner jacket. They would be in every single wedding picture, and there wasn't a thing Mom could do about it. Nor Denise.

Denise was a beautiful bride, with her long, dark hair in a cascade of ringlets beneath her veil and her full-skirted white brocade gown trailing behind her. I felt sad for her. She was passing from my parents' house to her husband's without ever getting a chance to live for herself.

I was not a bridesmaid but performed the music instead. I played "Here Comes the Bride" on the organ, and when Denise and Jerry snuffed out their individual candles and lit a big one together, I played my guitar and sang a song I had composed for the occasion, "Now We Are One." Candy Lambert had once said that when I sang I sounded like a bullfrog; another time like a mosquito. When I hit the final high note, Candy nudged Lisa and pointed at me. She opened her mouth wide, rolled back her eyes, and shook her jaw, causing Lisa to snicker. My voice tightened, forcing my vibrato to go out of control, making me sound something like a mosquito.

At the wedding reception in the church hall, the buffet table was packed with salads, relish dishes, and casseroles assembled by the members of Mom's garden club. I loaded my plate high, while Rena followed behind me, forming tiny islands of a few selected items, repulsed if different foods touched one another on her plate.

"Did you notice that Lisa and Candy are here?" Rena asked.

"Did I? Candy was making fun of me while I was trying to sing and made me goof up. Hopefully it's so crowded in here, we can avoid them."

"We'd sit with them if they asked us, right?"

"You can if you want," I snapped.

"It looks like Lisa got another nose job this summer."

"Yeah." Lisa was the only person I knew who had had plastic surgery. I didn't think her nose looked bad to begin with, just Italian, but the first surgery had left a little bump in it. Now nothing much was left but a pert little ski jump. She was also the only girl I knew whose mother let her get her hair bleached.

Rena and I found a good spot at a table and dug in, whispering hilarious observations about the wedding guests.

Suddenly Candy and Lisa were at our sides. "You sang real good," Candy said. She turned to Lisa, and they snickered together.

Lisa was pretty, except for her too-small nose and her blond hair that didn't match her olive complexion. Candy's features sank into a hollow at the center of her face, and she had a short bubble haircut that exposed puffy earlobes. I wondered if she would seem less ugly if she weren't so mean. I wondered why mean girls were popular.

Lisa was wearing the latest style, a white frilly blouse and a jumper that scooped beneath her bust line, emphasizing her big boobs. Candy was wearing a ribbed poor boy top, a tweed mod cap, and a brown wide-wale corduroy miniskirt, broader than it was long. I made a mental note to tell Rena later that Candy's bulging thighs in her mottled textured hose looked like sausages in casings. My mom wouldn't let me wear either outfit, claiming they wouldn't look good on me. I didn't understand this reasoning, knowing what every teen girl knows in her heart: the latest fashion looks good simply because it's the latest fashion.

"Pretty good eats," said Candy, nodding toward our plates. "We've got something that will make them taste even better!" She opened her clutch purse to reveal two joints, bulging and ineptly rolled. "Want to smoke some grass?"

My heart began to thump faster. Did Rena and I dare try pot *now*, on my sister's day of days, with two in-crowd kids I didn't trust? I had heard it was hard to inhale marijuana the first time. What if I was struck with a humiliating coughing fit?

"Since when do you smoke pot?" I asked. The in-crowd kids were drinkers, not dopers. At a football game last fall Lisa had gotten so drunk she'd vomited all over her flower-power tent dress and passed out. The story that got around school was that Kent had to scoop her up and toss her in the trunk of his dad's Cadillac to keep her from stinking up the interior. She came to while he was hosing her down in her backyard, before hoisting her through her bedroom window.

Candy put on her leering grin. "This summer I got a three-joint-a-day habit."

Alarms were sounding in my head. Pot users did not consider it a habit.

"I want to try it, Joanne," said Rena.

I looked around. My parents were still busy with the receiving line, greeting all their guests alongside Denise, Jerry, and his parents. It was stuffy in the crowded hall, and if we four girls slipped out, it would seem like we were going for some air.

We went out the side door, around the corner to the picnic tables. The outside lights weren't on in that area and the place was deserted.

Candy handed a joint to Rena.

"Don't you want the first hit?" Rena asked her.

"No, no. This grass is just for you guys. It might only be enough for two."

"Yeah," said Lisa. "Candy and I got stoned before the wedding and still have a buzz on."

Rena placed the joint between her lips, and Candy held a match to its end. It didn't catch.

"Suck harder," said Candy, lighting another match. "Haven't you ever done this before?"

"Lots of times." Rena inhaled so deeply, she began to sway and hyperventilate.

"You sure you've done this?" asked Lisa. "We gotta get back before my parents miss us."

"Let me try." I put the joint in my mouth; it was soggy from Rena. Candy handed Rena the matches, and she and Lisa left us fumbling in the dark. I tried so hard to light that joint, I wore it out. Grass started poking through the paper. Rena and I examined it.

"Hmmm, looks too green to burn," said Rena. "Doesn't it have to get dried out first?"

"Hey, wait." I held the joint under my nose and sniffed. "It's grass, all right." I bent over, yanked up a handful of lawn, and flung it at Rena in disgust.

In the dark, I could see Rena's eyes, drooping at the corners. "How are we going to live this one down?"

I laughed. Rena laughed. It was embarrassing, but it didn't hurt, not the way Candy's making fun of my singing did. As we walked back inside, I was relieved we hadn't smoked pot. I could have done something stupid, and then Denise would never have forgiven me for ruining her wedding.

During the bride and groom's dance, Denise and Jerry didn't stand apart from each other, stomp their feet, and wave their arms the way kids danced. They foxtrotted to "Blue Moon." Denise's left hand with the winking diamond ring was held high in Jerry's right hand, and his left hand lightly touched her waist. I hadn't known Denise could foxtrot, nor did I know where she had learned it. After a while my parents, Jerry's parents, and their friends joined in, Jerry and Denise fitting right in with the swirling, foxtrotting older couples. Denise no longer seemed a mere three years older than me, but somehow had advanced an entire generation. My sister was now one of *them*—a grown-up.

Later the DJ got around to spinning some of the songs of the current decade: The Troggs' "Wild Thing," the Monkees' "I'm a Believer," and the Turtles' "Happy Together." As Rena and I dug into our second pieces of wedding cake, the Doors' "Light My Fire" came on. I bounced to the beat of the music but froze when I felt a tap on my shoulder. I looked up to see Pete Wattle. He, Dan, and Jimmy Howe, who was now serving in Vietnam, had been buddies since junior high.

"Wanna dance?" asked Pete.

I did but had to consider who was asking. Pete was hilarious, always cracking jokes and pulling pranks. I had been laughed at enough for one day. "Buzz off."

His face was flushed from the champagne he and my brother had been helping themselves to, but he still seemed steady on his feet. "No, really. I want to dance with you."

"Why?" I asked suspiciously.

"Why? Because this song is far out!" He grinned, exposing the cute gap between his two front teeth. He had grown his blond hair out and swept it across his forehead, surfer boy style. His acne had cleared up, and he'd lost or grown into his baby fat. He actually looked pretty cool.

If I got up to dance with Pete, Rena would be left alone. She leaned into me and whispered, "Say you'll do it if Dan will dance with me."

I relayed the message to Pete, and by the organ solo of "Light My Fire," the four of us were doing some heavy-duty rocking out. Pete was a pretty good dancer, or at least he didn't look like he was spazzing out, like Dan. I closed my eyes and felt the music seeping into my brain, the beat pulsing deep in my bones, and the release of all the tension brought on by the wedding. The song changed to the Airplane's "Somebody to Love." I kicked off my high heels and spun around in stocking feet. My steps grew wider, and soon I was leaping across the dance floor.

Pete jogged after me, his face crumpled with frustration. "Don't be hopping all over the place, Joanne."

I ignored his pleas, and he soon gave up on my galloping, sashaying, and weaving. I was alone in the music, flying high, Grace Slick wailing, "Don't you want somebody to love? Don't you need somebody to love?" Yeah, I did, and I thought of my beautiful hippie.

After that song, Rena and I flopped, sweaty and panting, at a table next to her parents.

"Your mom did a wonderful job on this wedding," said Mrs. Thompson.

"Thanks. I'll tell her you said so."

"And Denise was a beautiful, blushing bride. A girl's wedding day is the most important day of her life," gushed Mrs. Thompson.

"Yeah, right," said Mr. Thompson, "and a marriage certificate is a man's death warrant."

Mrs. Thompson gave him a wide-eyed, wounded look as he stared blandly back. Her face shattered like glass, and she ran out of the room.

"That was really mean, Dad," said Rena.

"Ah, hell. Come on, Rena. We're going."

"It's early. I can walk home."

He stood. "We're going," he repeated, and headed for the door, not even bothering to turn around to see if Rena was following.

Rena raised a peace sign at me, more like a sign of surrender than a farewell.

Left alone, I reached for a handful of chocolate-covered mint patties; then, realizing I was too stuffed to eat another bite, I stashed them in my satin clutch purse for later. I would forget about them, they would melt into the lining, and after that, every time I opened that purse, I would smell mint and be transported back to Denise's wedding day.

Mom's friend Maxine Fulmer came over to talk to me. I knew she was there because I had seen her untouched sunflower seed tofu loaf in its disposable aluminum baking pan, parked among all the polished silver serving dishes on the buffet table. She had brought a guest, a thin, pale man with a pageboy who looked quite a bit younger than her and reminded me of Chopin.

Mrs. Fulmer introduced him to me as Quentin Allen. He extended his hand across the table, and when I shook it, I noticed how good his long, pale fingers would be for piano playing. Whenever I didn't know what to say to somebody, I said something stupid to fill the silence. "I've never met anyone whose name starts with a 'Q.'"

"What's more unusual is someone whose name starts with 'Q' but without a 'u' following it. Now, that's impressive."

"Is that even possible?"

"Qadir, Qamar, Qihael. Need I go on?" He smiled with one side of his mouth, which made him boyishly handsome. He extracted a gold cigarette case from his hunter-green velveteen jacket, snapped it open, and offered its contents to me. I declined but was flattered. I'd never been offered a cigarette before.

"I've been looking for you, Joanne," said Mrs. Fulmer, her speech slightly slurred from the champagne she was sipping. "I just had to compliment your music at the ceremony. You play with such feeling. Such expression. Truly, it's a gift."

"Thank you, Mrs. Fulmer."

"Call me Maxine, dear. These titles alienate the generations, don't you think? Besides, I'm not even Mrs. Fulmer anymore."

I asked Maxine a question I probably shouldn't. "Do weddings make you sad?"

"This one does. Denise is much too young. Too bad she and Jerry couldn't just live together for a while."

I was shocked that a person of my parents' generation would suggest such a thing. "You know my mom wouldn't go for that."

"It's becoming widely accepted," Maxine insisted. "Denise will see it's not easy for a girl to return to college once she's left. She's been brainwashed into thinking getting married and having children will make her a happy, feminine, well-adjusted woman with a fulfilling sex life. Society says education for girls only dooms them to unhappy, dead-end careers and celibate, frustrated lives without orgasm." I was embarrassed by her anger and sex talk, especially in the presence of a man. I didn't know what "orgasm" meant. Everything I knew about sex I'd learned by secretly reading *Valley of the Dolls* while babysitting, and parts of it I didn't understand.

"Girls don't dare become interested in law and medicine," Maxine ranted on. "It will only lead to the frustration of applying for positions filled by men. No, no. Teach them cooking and sewing and"—she clawed quotation marks in the air—"'the role of woman in society.' I read in Betty Friedan's *The Feminine Mystique* that in the last decade, the IQs of teenage girls in America have actually gone *down*!"

I thought of Denise in junior high, reading one book after another—Dickens, Austen, J. D. Salinger, Joyce Carol Oates— and then in the summer before her freshman year, something happened to her. She grew boobs, big pointy ones, and all her dates and hair arranging put a limit on her reading.

"Keep 'em barefoot and pregnant," Maxine muttered.

"Oh, no, not Jerry!" I said, defending my new brother-in-law, whom I liked so much. I leaned close to Maxine to whisper their secret. "Denise is on the Pill."

"So she can support *him*," Maxine almost snarled. "That's the other subject they teach you girls in high school, isn't it? Typing—so you can support a man attending a university for a real profession, so you can type *his* dissertation instead of writing your own. That's what those male chauvinist *pigs* want, and they always get what they want!" She stopped, nearly panting.

If Quentin was insulted by her talk, he didn't show it. He smoked his cigarette, putting a lot of wrist motion in it and following through with a sweep of his arm. He was the most stylish smoker I'd ever seen.

# CHAPTER FIVE

On Thursday nights my parents went out to dinner and on to their ballroom dance lessons. It used to be a treat for Denise, Dan, and me to eat TV dinners on trays in front of the boob tube watching *The Mod Squad*, but now, with Denise married and Dan off at his new pizza delivery job, Thursday nights were even better. I had the whole house to myself to practice the piano as loudly and long as I wanted. But that night was special. I was going to sneak off to Martin's with Rena.

My parents left the house at five-thirty, and I waited a full ten minutes before charging down to Walker Street to Rena's house.

When she opened the door, she seemed surprised to see me. "Oh, Jo! I forgot! I can't go!"

"Why not?"

"Look, I'll show you! It's fantastic!" She led me into her living room and opened the pink entertainment section of the *San Francisco Chronicle*. "The American Conservatory Theater is casting *The Crucible,* and they're having auditions tonight! It's about the Salem witch trials, and they need a bunch of teenage girls to spaz out and act like they're possessed by the devil. I've been rehearsing all afternoon. Watch!" Rena rolled her eyes and jerked her arms around, then dropped in a heap to the floor as if her skeleton had dissolved to Jell-O. She sat up with a grin. "Pretty convincing, huh?"

"Yeah, but you promised you'd come with me."

"I know, Jo. I'm sorry. Can't you go alone?"

I hugged myself. "I'd be too scared without you."

"We'll go tomorrow!" Rena said brightly.

But I was psyched up to go right then. I had selected the perfect outfit. I had rehearsed all the cool things I'd say to Martin. I started to trudge home, but when I got to Ashbury, I turned left toward Haight.

I passed a couple of scary-looking Hells Angels astride their Harley choppers. I was pretty certain the one with scraggly hair, a black beard, and a beer gut was the famous Chocolate George. He wore a denim shirt with the sleeves ripped out as a vest, dotted with peace buttons. My eyes slid away from him, and I walked a little faster. The Hells Angels had once held the entire town of Hollister hostage, and even more terrifying, they had been prosecuted for gang rape. Dozens of Hells Angels had rolled into the Haight and decided to hang around and drop acid. They seemed peaceful enough, but still they made me nervous.

I sat at the trolley stop, and when it arrived, I got on. Every fiber of my being told me not to do this. Every newspaper clipping about abduction, rape, and murder that my mother had ever read aloud to me rose in giant letters in my mind. Simply, I would be killed, and it served me right because when my parents went out, they trusted me to stay home with my TV dinner and piano.

When the trolley stopped at Beach Street, I got off. I walked across the street, through the gate, and up the steep, cracked walkway to Martin's house. A recording of the Purple Cockroach's "Evolution! Revolution!" blared from an open basement window. I knocked and waited, but no one answered. Maybe Martin was watching me from behind the curtains, not really wanting me to visit and waiting for me to leave. This thought caused me to dash down the walkway. Soon I'd be on the trolley rumbling home, safe and sound.

When I got to the street again, the music abruptly stopped in the middle of the tune. I realized that maybe my knock couldn't be heard and I should try again. But by the time I made it through the gate and up the walkway a second time, the music had started at the second verse, as if the needle of the phonograph had been dropped in the middle of the record. This time I knocked more loudly.

The music halted, and out of the basement came a long string of obscenities in a booming male voice. It didn't sound like Martin, and whoever it was sounded really pissed off. I took off at a run.

Behind me, I heard the door swing open. "You!" boomed the angry voice. "What the fuck do you want?"

I turned. A man in a full beard, long hair, and rainbow suspenders was leaping off the porch toward me.

"Oh! It *is* you!" I cried, my hand flying to my mouth. Rena had been right! It was no recording I'd heard, but the real thing, the Purple Cockroach live, in rehearsal.

Gus Abbott was smiling at me now, flattered that he had been recognized. I must have looked like a scared, dumbfounded teenybopper. I *was* a scared, dumbfounded teenybopper. "How'd you find out we live here?" he asked.

"I . . . I didn't."

"Then who are you looking for?"

I pointed behind him. Martin was loping down the porch steps. I looked from Gus to Martin and back again. Even with Gus's beard, I could see the family resemblance.

"Hi, Joni," said Martin. He hugged me as Gus went back into the house.

"You're brothers? You and Gus Abbott?"

"Uh-huh."

"You *live* with the Purple Cockroach?"

He rattled his finger around in his ear. "Gets kinda noisy sometimes."

"But it's so far out! You get to hear them all the time!"

He rolled his eyes. "Too much. They're trying to get enough material together for an album." He put his arm around my shoulder. "Come on in. I'll make us some dinner."

He led me to a yellow kitchen with flowers painted all over

the walls and a dozen suncatchers hanging in the window over the sink. From one of the glass-paned cupboards, he removed a loaf of bread and a jar of peanut butter.

I laughed.

"What?" he said. "This is the perfect dinner! Chock-full of crunchy protein, and only forty-nine cents a jar." He lifted the loaf of wheat bread. "A man can live a week on this and live well."

"What about jelly?"

From the refrigerator he extracted strawberry jam, my favorite, and smeared one of the pieces of bread with it. "I prefer my peanut butter in the nude, but in celebration of a dinner guest, I'll add a little jam to my sandwich, too." He wiped the knife clean on another piece of bread before dipping it into the peanut butter. He wrapped the sandwiches in waxed paper and stuck them in a backpack along with a canteen of water. "We can't eat such an elegant dinner in such humble surroundings. Let's go."

Together we walked down Beach Street, past the marina, and through the Presidio, talking as we went. I told him I had lived my whole life in the same house on Frederick Street, and he said he and Gus had lived with Max and Vivian all over the world: the Florida Keys, Majorca, Casablanca, and Bennington, Vermont.

"Are Max and Vivian your parents?" I asked.

He frowned. "They're Max and Vivian. Anyways, in January me and Gus came out here for the Human Be-In in Golden Gate Park, liked the vibes, and decided to stick around for a while. Gus put Roach together, but I'm a vagabond. One day you'll see me here, next day I'll be gone to Timbuktu."

It was disappointing to think of Martin leaving just as I was getting to know him. "I've heard of Timbuktu, but I don't know where it is."

"Mali." He looked out across the expanse of the ocean. "My head is really into this place for now."

"How old are you?" I blurted.

"Is age important?"

"No," I said, thinking that was the cool answer. But why should I say what I thought he wanted to hear, when I believed he could understand the real me? I needed to be myself, but that was an act of bravery. "Age is kinda important," I admitted tentatively. "Like, my dad is forty-six, and if you were in your forties it would be too weird, like there'd be the generation gap between us."

He laughed. "I'm not even in my twenties. But I don't believe in the generation gap. There's hip people of all ages."

"I haven't met too many." My new piano teacher, Dr. Harold, was cool, and I decided Maxine was, too. It was strange to think of a friend of my mom's as being with-it. Martin got me thinking about a lot of things.

When we reached the Golden Gate Bridge, I hesitated. "We're going to *walk* across the bridge?" I had never thought to do that. Maybe it was because my mother had read me too many newspaper articles about people jumping off.

"You look freaked out," said Martin.

"No! I mean...kinda."

"Come on, lady." He took my hand. As we walked, our arms swung lightly between us. The sea breeze whipped our hair into our mouths, and the sun sinking over the hills painted the water gold and magenta. I forgot about jumping off the bridge or falling, because now Martin held my hand.

We sat on the sandy Marin headlands, shoulder pressed to shoulder, watching a massive cruise ship, freighters, fishing rigs, and sailboats drift by.

"I used to think 'Golden Gate' was the name given to the bridge," I said, "but then I found out the entrance of the bay was called that before the bridge was here. I think of all those Oriental people sailing, sailing, sailing on the Pacific, and then finally they get here to pass through the Golden Gate."

"You've given me an idea," Martin said. "I'm going to look for photographs of what it looked like before the bridge was built."

The wind caught our hair and wove it together. I tried to hook mine behind my ear so I could see, and pulled some of Martin's. We laughed together.

He took the peanut butter sandwiches out of the pack and offered me one. I was ravenous and took a huge bite.

"Chew," he said.

"I am."

"Chew more. Don't swallow any of those little chunks of peanut without grinding all the goodness out of them." He took the canteen out of his backpack and offered it to me. "Here, drink. The best beverage in the world."

The water did taste especially fresh and sweet. "Are you a health food nut?"

"I enjoy good, simple food. 'Simplify! Simplify! Simplify!' That's a quote."

I rolled my eyes toward him. "That's a word."

"When it's said thrice, it's a quote."

"Thrice? Nobody says 'thrice.'"

"You've never heard anyone say 'thrice'? How old are you?"

Too young for him, probably. I cocked my head and looked at him out of the corner of my eye. "Age isn't important, is it?"

"Just tell me."

"I'm not even twenty yet."

He laughed. "You're a wiseass, Joni. An old soul."

"Oh! You're a Buddhist?"

"Naw, Buddhists think it's a terrible fate to be kicked back into another life, and I love life so I can't be one of them. I don't believe in reincarnation, but isn't 'old soul' a beautiful expression?"

"That's what some people say about Mozart. Since he could play and compose like an adult, as a child, he lived previous lives."

"Is that what you think?"

"Naw, I'm an Episcopalian."

"What's that?"

"Don't exactly know, but they stick plastic Jesuses into plaster of Paris. Do you go to church?"

"Naw. But I'm very spiritual."

"What religion?"

"Hmmm, Transcendentalist, I guess."

I had not heard of Transcendentalists, but I had heard of Transcendental Meditation, like what the Beatles were into. "Oh! Who's your guru?"

His laugh came out like a hoot. "My guru? Henry David Thoreau!"

"The Walden Pond guy, who lived his whole life in a log cabin?"

"Just two years." He shook his head. "Nothing to sustain it. Like this party going on here, the whole Hashbury hippie scene."

"My brother Dan thinks hippies are a Communist plot. I can't believe I'm sitting here right now with a hippie!"

"Where?" Martin looked around him. "What's a hippie?"

"A bum with long hair and bad hygiene!" I laughed. "That's my dad's definition."

"I take regular showers. What's your definition?"

For over two years, I'd lived among hippies. I thought I knew exactly what one was, but it was hard to explain. "Someone who gets to do exactly what he wants to do and doesn't care what people—older people, society—say about him."

"Don't all people do what they want?"

"No. Some of us have to go to school and work."

"Don't you want to?"

I saw what he meant. I wouldn't want to be a high school dropout, so I guessed I wanted to be in school. "Have you taken a lot of drugs?"

He shrugged. "Some. I was a caffeine addict, but I went cold turkey."

"Never heard of it."

"It's an upper, in coffee and Coke. Bad stuff. Made my hands shake and my heart race. Now I just drink chamomile and mint tea. My own blend."

"I'd like to try grass," I said timidly.

"I'll turn you on sometime."

I was thrilled by the idea, not just because I'd finally get to smoke pot, but because Martin seemed to indicate that he wanted to see me again.

"Do you smoke a lot of dope?"

He shook his head. "Moderation. That's where my head's at."

"I'd like to try LSD, but the idea freaks me out."

"Acid freaks a lot of people out. It's not meant to party with, I don't think." He dangled his fingers and shook them. "Far out, man, look at all the pretty lights and colors," he said in a high, spacy tone, then returned to his own voice. "I don't go as far as Timothy Leary, who calls dropping acid a religion, but it is a soul-searching, mind-tripping thing."

"I've read about Leary's church—the League of Spiritual Discovery."

He shrugged. "Uh-huh. He preaches against 'nonsacramental' use. But it's more psychological than spiritual. It's a head trip, and if you're afraid of what you might find in your own head, you'll freak out. You gotta have your shit together."

I had never heard that expression. I imagined turds in a toilet. I had heard of people jumping out of windows, tripping on LSD and thinking they could fly. I looked out at the bridge, imagining myself taking a swan dive off it. I shuddered.

"I'm glad I'm beyond acid," Martin said.

"Huh?"

He smiled. "I've found it's just the same after a few times. I'm not going to learn anything else by doing more. Sure, it's beautiful—a good trip is. The mind expands to show you a million possibilities. You feel 'one' with everybody. There's an amazing awareness of the beauty of the world. But then you come down. Every time, you come down, and you're the same, with your same problems." He swept his arm across the expanse of the headlands, the bay, the city. "Look at this place. Why go mind-tripping and come back thinking it's not as good as before you left it? Bummer!"

"I still want to try it once."

"Then do it."

The sky was completely dark when we made our way back, but the steady stream of cars across the bridge lit our way. It was still early, around nine, and I knew I could sneak home before my parents returned. Martin gave me a long hug good-bye.

"It was good rapping with you," he said.

"Thanks for dinner."

I looked deep into his lovely eyes, searching for something to take away with me. I hoped he would offer some future plans, but he merely whispered, "Peace," his breath warm on my ear. Then he was gone, across the street and behind the gate, leaving me alone in the dark, hoping some Hells Angels gang rapists wouldn't come along before my trolley did.

Even as the streetcar rattled across town, I was far from peace. I was already gone, gone, gone on Martin, and yet he had not even mentioned getting together again. We had talked about a lot of things, but he was as mysterious as ever. What next?

I was bursting to tell Rena my news, but it was too confidential to report over the phone with my mother possibly listening in. The next afternoon Rena and I got away for a walk in Golden Gate Park. I thought there couldn't be anything more exciting than my visit with Martin and meeting Gus Abbott of Roach, but Rena assumed her news was more important than mine.

She had landed the part of Susanna Walcott in the ACT production of *The Crucible*. "I've got six lines," she said proudly, "and some of the girls don't have any. In the courtroom scene we pretend Mary Warren is possessing us, and I say, 'Her claws! She's stretching her claws!'" She raised her arms and bent her fingers, ducking her head fearfully. I was getting worn out, waiting for my turn to talk. Finally she asked, "Did you go see that hippie guy?" I started to tell my story and she blurted, "I knew it was Gus Abbott! Your boyfriend is his brother? Far out!"

"He's not my boyfriend!"

"Well, you went on a date."

"Not really a date. We just went for a walk and rapped."

"You rapped?"

I laughed at the way Rena screwed up her face, as if I had just confessed an obscene act. "That's what Martin calls talking."

"That's so funny! Does Roach all live together in one house like the Grateful Dead?"

"I don't know. But it's a big house. It seems like lots of people live there."

"Oh, take me to meet Gus!" Rena jumped in front of me, clasped her palms together, and pretended to flop to her knees.

"Sure." I didn't want to talk about Roach. I wanted to talk about Martin. I began again and Rena interrupted again.

"Did you find out how old he is?"

"He said age didn't matter, that we're all just people."

"What school does he go to?"

"None."

"Then he is old! Did he try to make love to you right there on the beach?"

"Rena, no! Keep it down!" I exclaimed in shock, looking around to see if anyone had overheard her loud, dramatic voice. "He didn't even kiss me. I wanted him to, but we just talked. He knows a lot."

"Maybe he was homeschooled. Homeschoolers get to think what they want, not the way teachers say we're supposed to. I may need to be homeschooled if my acting career takes off."

Six lines in a play didn't sound like stardom to me, but I didn't say so.

"Just wait until Candy and Lisa and those guys find out I'm a professional actress with ACT and you're friends with Gus Abbott."

I stopped and clutched her arms. "Oh! We can't tell them! If it gets back to my mother she'll stop me from seeing Martin!"

"Oh, right. Hey, Jo, maybe sometime we can go hear Roach at the Fillmore or the Avalon."

Those dance halls were famous for the Acid Tests that took place before October 6, 1966, the day LSD became illegal. Vats of Kool-Aid laced with acid had been offered to hundreds of people at a time, but now the trips were merely staged with light shows and psychedelic rock. Big-name bands like Big Brother and the Holding Company and Quicksilver Messenger Service were still featured at the dances, but you had to be eighteen to get in.

"It will be hard not to tell," said Rena, still thinking about her role. "I want to brag to everybody."

"I'm just happy inside. Ever notice how if you tell something really good that happened to you to somebody who doesn't care about you, it doesn't seem as good to you anymore? I tried so hard to be popular last year, and Candy Lambert made fun of me so many times."

"Do you think kids would think she's funny if she wasn't Candy Lambert?"

"Who cares? The person I was trying to be the last two years wasn't me at all. This year I'm just going to be myself and not care what anybody thinks."

"It's not that easy," said Rena, her eyebrows scrunched together. "When I saw Lisa and Candy at Denise's wedding, I hated them and was dying to impress them at the same time."

At least Rena and I had each other. Since we couldn't share our far-out news with anyone else, we developed a code to remind each other about it. Whenever we met or talked on the phone, Rena would say, "Her claws! She's stretching her claws!" and I'd reply, "Rap, rap."

# CHAPTER
# SIX

"No wisecracks about her cooking, Dan," said Mom from the front seat as Dad steered our blue Oldsmobile sedan over the Bay Bridge toward Berkeley. It was a Saturday night, and we were in our Sunday best. With her pink polyester knit dress, Mom wore a pillbox hat with a half veil and carried matching short gloves. Dad was in a business suit and tie. I felt sorry for my parents. They were so old they had nothing exciting to look forward to. Still, they seemed happy enough.

"I'll eat anything," said Dan, who rode in the backseat with me. He had on slacks and a dress shirt. I wore my new plaid wool skirt that had a giant brass safety pin on the side, with a frilly white blouse, a scarf, and heels. It was a lot of effort to get on all that gear just to visit Denise and Jerry, but we always dressed up to go out to dinner.

"No rude comments," said Mom. "I don't want to see your sister in tears the first time she entertains us as a married woman."

"Who can wreck spaghetti?" asked Dan.

"It's not as easy as it looks," said Dad. "If you overcook the noodles, they turn to glue."

"Which is why we're going to be a half hour early. So I can oversee the operation," said Mom. Poor Denise. She didn't have a chance in hell of running her own show.

Denise greeted us at the door of the tiny walk-up apartment, her face glowing with pride. Beneath her apron she wore an empire-waisted, floor-length floral-print cotton gown, with long sleeves that were puffed at the shoulders, a new fashion called a granny dress. Her long hair was drawn back by a leather headband across her forehead, and beneath her hem, pale pink ballet slippers peeked out.

"How can you even walk in that thing?" Dad kissed her on the cheek and handed her a huge fruit basket as a housewarming present.

"Where're your real shoes?" Mom asked. "Those tight things will give you corns."

"Something smells great," said Dan.

Jerry came out of the back of the apartment. Dad extended his hand to shake, and his eyes popped when Jerry hugged him. Jerry hugged Mom and me, but Dan stepped behind me, safely out of man-hugging range. Jerry wore hip-hugger white denim bell-bottoms and a fringed suede vest with his usual Oxford button-down shirt and wing-tip shoes. During the three weeks since the wedding his hair had grown even shaggier. I wanted to laugh at his half-straight, half-hip look.

I'd been to the apartment the week before the wedding, when Mom was helping Denise furnish it and set up housekeeping. Now it seemed more cramped than ever, with fondue pots, chip-and-dip layered bowls, vases, crystal ashtrays, and silver serving pieces covering every surface in the living room. It would be a tight fit for the six of us to crowd around the kitchen table.

"What can I do to help, Denise?"

"Not a thing, Mother. Everything's about ready. Come into the living room and Jerry will make you a highball."

Mom turned a full circle in the center of the tiny kitchen. There was no evidence of meal preparations, except that on the clean counter stood a tossed salad, a loaf of sourdough bread on a cutting board, and an iced chocolate cake. "What about the—"

"The lasagna is in the oven," said Denise, bouncing on the balls of her feet.

"Lasagna! Oh, boy!" said Dan, clapping his hands. "Mom never makes that anymore." He followed Dad into the living room, where Denise had set out chips and dips.

"Lasagna is so complicated," said Mom. "You shouldn't have gone to the trouble, Denise. How did you ever learn to make it?"

"I just followed the recipe."

"Recipes don't teach you how to cook. You need someone who . . ." Mom's voice trailed off as she gazed at the table set with an avocado-green tablecloth to match Denise's new Desert Rose Franciscan dinnerware. "A tablecloth *and* cloth napkins? Candles, too? You shouldn't have gone to the trouble just for us."

"She uses them every night," Jerry said proudly, ringing Denise's waist with his arm. "They're so much nicer than place mats and paper napkins. And candles are so romantic." He kissed her right in front of us. "Oh, honey, run down to our garage locker, will you? Get the other bourbon for us."

Denise swung the apron over her head and hiked up her dress, ready to take two flights of stairs in her ballet slippers. Her exit from the apartment gave Mom the opportunity to peek into the oven at the bubbling lasagna. She looked over her shoulder and hastily salted the dish before snapping the oven shut. "Those recipes never say to boil the noodles a few minutes first," she told me. "We'll be chewing all night. I just hope we can get it down and spare Denise's feelings."

It was the best lasagna I'd ever eaten, maybe because Denise used real ricotta, while Mom cut corners with cottage cheese.

Over coffee, the men in the living room argued about the U.S. getting out of the United Nations, Dan in favor of the idea and Dad and Jerry against it, while Mom, helping Denise with the dishes in the kitchen, tried to convince her that ironing the bedsheets and Jerry's boxer shorts was unnecessary.

"That's the way Jerry likes them," said Denise. "That's the way his mother and his aunt did things."

"Humph." Mom reared back her chin.

I had no position in either debate, so I slipped away to the bathroom. It was decorated with furry pink throw rugs and a matching furry pink toilet seat cover with just-for-show pink shell-shaped soaps in an abalone dish.

Coming out of the bathroom, I noticed the looming double bed that nearly filled the only bedroom. Three weeks ago, my sister and I had lain side by side in matching twin beds, and now she slept in a full bed with a *man*. He probably saw her naked. She probably saw him. They did *it*. What did it feel like? Did she like it? Love it? Couldn't get enough? I'd never know. Denise wasn't one to talk about such things.

I was embarrassed to think such thoughts and avoided looking at Jerry when I returned to the living room. I picked up the *Time* magazine with the Generation Gap cover and retreated to the corner of the room. I didn't have to read an article to know that my parents' generation and my generation were like two alien nations who didn't speak the same language but shared the same planet. I just wanted to go home and get my itchy skirt and tight girdle off.

In the car, Mom commented on Denise cluttering up her counter with her mushroom-patterned flour, sugar, and tea canister set instead of keeping them in the cupboard. "And she'll soon realize doing up a tablecloth and napkins is just too much work."

"The lasagna was great," said Dan.

Mother patted her bosom with the heel of her fist. "I just hope I don't get heartburn from all those onions in the sauce."

"Coffee was good," said Dad. "Plenty strong."

Mother glared over at him. "I suppose mine is too weak."

Suddenly we realized the trouble Mom was in and rushed to her defense.

"Your spaghetti sauce is a lot better," said Dan.

"And the lasagna was too salty," said Dad.

"Not salty enough," I said.

"And the cake was obviously from a mix," said Dad. "Can't beat your cakes from scratch, dear."

"And that tablecloth was ostentatious," I said.

"Austin who?" asked Dad. He liked to be funny like that.

"Now, now, don't you all be so hard on Denise," said Mom

with a prim smile. "Setting up housekeeping isn't easy. She'll find her way. And she and Jerry seem *very* happy."

"That's all that matters," said Dad.

Mom nodded but couldn't resist having the last say. "That husband of hers needs a haircut if he ever expects the professional world to take him seriously."

# CHAPTER
# SEVEN

Whenever I wanted to do something I knew my mother wouldn't allow, I quietly bought or collected the materials and waited for her to leave the house. One afternoon when she was at her garden club luncheon, I went out into the backyard to tie-dye a T-shirt, following the directions I found in *Teen* magazine. I had bought a plain white Fruit of the Loom small men's T-shirt, which I wadded up in sections and secured with rubber bands. Then I put another rubber band a little farther up on each clump. Next I mixed up packages of yellow, red, and violet Rit dye and put each color in a spray bottle. I sprayed the different colors over each part of the T-shirt that was sectioned off by the rubber bands. Finally I cut the rubber bands, and out came groovy sunbursts of color all over the T-shirt. It was really fun and easy, and I was proud of my creation.

Just as I was hanging it up on the clothesline to dry, Mom appeared at the French doors, home from her luncheon. She crossed her arms and yelled, "You can't be trusted home alone for two little hours, Joanne. If you think you're going out in public in hippie clothes, you've got another thing coming."

When she went back into the house, I smiled to myself. I'd gotten my tie-dye T-shirt, and she couldn't stop me from wearing it.

\* \* \*

Two days later when Mom went to Safeway for her week's grocery shopping, I put on my tie-dye T-shirt, my bell-bottoms, sandals, love beads, and peace button. All the cool girls were buying their Levi's in the men's department because they didn't make jeans for girls that rode on the hips. Of course my mother wouldn't let me do this, but no one knew that beneath my tie-dye T-shirt the waistband of my homemade bell-bottoms hit me two inches above my belly button. I had washed my long, brown hair over and over so that it was straight and flyaway. I applied colorless lip gloss, blusher, and a hint of mascara on individual lashes so it all looked natural. Then I went roaming around the neighborhood looking for Martin.

I found him on Hippie Hill, a sloping, broad meadow in Golden Gate Park, not far from the Stanyan Street entrance, bordered on two sides with eucalyptus. Dozens of flower children were sitting in clusters, lying back sunning themselves, rapping, and smoking weed. It would not seem odd or forward for me to join any of these groups, even if I didn't know a single person among them.

Martin was sitting off alone, playing his guitar. He paused in his singing to smile up at me and say, "Peace." He seemed happy to see me.

I sat cross-legged opposite him. "Go on. I want to hear the rest of the song." It was one I'd never heard before, about revolving things: windmills, carousels, wheels, and the earth. When he finished, I clapped. "That's beautiful! Who recorded it?"

"No one. I wrote it."

"Wow! You should record it. You could be as famous as Gus."

He laughed. "I don't want to be famous."

"What? Everyone wants to be famous!"

"Why?"

That simple question stumped me for a moment. For recognition. For acceptance. To prove to your family and the people you knew that you were a somebody. To prove to yourself that you were good at something. "Well, I want to be famous."

"Then that's how we're different, Joni."

His words stung. I didn't want Martin and me to have any

differences. I felt ashamed, like I was an egomaniac just because I wished for success. "Well, then, what do you want to do with your life?"

"Do with it?" He blinked incredulously. "Why, live it!"

"But what do you want to accomplish?"

"Not a blessed thing. Ambition destroys lives."

"Not in the arts."

"Of course in the arts!" His brow creased in agitation. "Believe me, I know what I'm talking about. Max is a playwright, and Vivian is a sculptor."

"Did Max ever get anything produced on Broadway?"

"Maybe off-off-*off*-Broadway. He just writes gibberish."

"Do you mean theater of the absurd?"

"No, I mean gibberish."

"Come on, Martin. Everyone wants to achieve something."

He straightened his spine and struck his chest, proclaiming, "Then I shall become a master liver of life!" We laughed together, and I was relieved that things had lightened up. He gave me an appreciative look. "That's a groovy shirt."

"Oh, thanks. I made it!"

"You look good in it." He extended his guitar toward me. "Here. If you're gonna be famous, you better practice. Play me something."

I shrank away. "Oh, I just sing and play the guitar for fun. Classical piano is what I work at."

"And it's not fun?"

"I love it. It's my life, but I wouldn't call it fun. Hmm...fulfilling, I guess."

"Heavy." He set his guitar in my lap. "Let's see what you can do with this."

I thought of Candy mocking my performance at Denise's wedding. "This girl in my school says I sound like a mosquito and a bullfrog."

"You must have a hell of a range."

That made me laugh. I wasn't at all nervous playing for Martin. I began a simple bass-chord-chord accompaniment pattern leading into "Little Boxes." It's about how houses all look the same, and the people in the houses are all the same, too, going to college, golfing, and drinking their martinis dry. As I played and sang, I looked into Martin's eyes. They crinkled at the corners when Malvina Reynolds's clever lyrics amused him.

"You are, too, good! I can tell you feel music deep down." He pressed his hand against his sternum. "It just pours out."

His praise embarrassed me. Embarrassment made me blush, and blushing embarrassed me more. I commented on the song. "I like it because it's against conformity."

"You're against conformity?"

Wasn't that obvious by what I was wearing and what I talked about? "Well, yeah."

"You're not going to grow up, get married, buy the car and the house with the white picket fence, and have two-point-two children?"

Of course I wanted to have a family, but way in the future. Martin was grinning at me like he had caught me in an inconsistency. "I don't know anybody with a white picket fence."

He laughed at me, but not in a mean way.

"Well, don't you want to get married and have kids someday?" I asked.

"Nope."

"Oh." My heart seemed to plunge to my stomach. "Not ever?"

"Never, ever. I'm going to be as free as a bird." He reclaimed his guitar. "Let's sing together, Joni. What will it be?"

I blurted the title of the first song that came to my mind. "'Blowin' in the Wind'?"

"Beautiful. Want to take harmony or melody?"

"Melody."

Martin didn't sing a third below me; instead, his bell-like tenor soared above my melody in an improvised, free-flowing countermelody. In her robust alto, Mary sometimes sang a part lower than Peter and Paul, and I liked the idea that the girl didn't always have to sing the high part. Our voices blended well.

I wanted to sit there forever, singing with Martin and basking in his warm glow.

"Joanne! What are you doing?" growled a gruff male voice, which I recognized before I even turned around. "Get home, now!"

Martin stopped strumming his guitar, and we both stared up at Dan, with Pete beside him.

"Why? I'm not doing anything wrong. Leave me alone." I turned back to Martin, rolling my eyes in exasperation.

Dan attempted to lift me by the armpits, and when I bore down, he began dragging me away. I kicked at him a few times, but not wanting to make a scene in front of Martin, I stopped resisting. I stood and twisted free of Dan's grip. "You're not the boss of me."

"Peace, brother," said Martin.

"I'm not your brother, you filthy hippie!" yelled Dan, stooping to flex his bicep in Martin's face. "I'm *her* brother, out to protect her from degenerates like you. Stay away from my sister or I'll have to pound you!" Dan gripped my upper arm and yanked me along. I was so humiliated I couldn't bear to look back at Martin, even to say good-bye.

"Are you in trouble, Joanne," said Dan. "Wait till I tell Mom where I found you and who you were with. Are you crazy? You could've been raped."

"Man, I don't think so," said Pete. "Those hippie chicks put out, like, all the time. Like, without a struggle," he clarified. Pete was funny like that.

"That right?" asked Dan. "Maybe we could disguise ourselves as hippies, go to a love-in, and get some ourselves." Dan always talked about sex as a dirty deed with an anonymous partner, rather than an expression of love between two people who cared for each other. "We can get some crabs or the clap. That's what those filthy hippie chicks put out."

I stopped short, darted behind Dan, and gave him a shove. My adrenaline must've been raging, because I pushed him so hard he stumbled forward, nearly falling on his face.

"You little bitch!" He grabbed my hair, wrapped it around his fist, and gave it a painful yank. I kicked him in the shin so that he had to let go of my hair to rub his leg and hop around. He raised an open palm to slap my face, and I cringed, bracing myself for the sting, which didn't come. Pete had caught his arm midair.

"Cool it, you guys." Pete didn't understand knock-down, drag-out sibling rivalry, having only one brother, a twenty-four-year-old Mongoloid who filled in his Flintstones coloring book and made jewelry boxes with Popsicle sticks and Elmer's glue.

Waiting for the light at Stanyan Street, I glanced behind me, fearful that Martin had followed us out of the park. What would he think of me? I glanced down at my peace button. I glared up at Dan through narrowed eyes. "I'm telling Mom you called me a bitch."

The light changed, and we started across the street.

"Don't, Joanne." Dan's eyes slid nervously from side to side. What he really meant was don't tell *Dad*. Not even I wished the consequences of that on Dan.

"Then don't tell Mom where you found me."

"I got to. She sent me looking for you, and she'll want to know. I ain't gonna lie for you."

"You don't have to tell her if she doesn't ask."

"All right, deal."

As we walked up Frederick Street, Dad was just driving home from work. He got out of the car to open the gate to our driveway. His tie was loosened and his face was flushed, indicating he'd had a hard day. This was going to be bad. He drove through the gate, and Dan rushed up to shut it for him. Pete raised his hand in farewell and continued up the street toward his house on West Buena Vista. Watching two Donnellys fight was scary enough; four was more than he could handle.

Usually when Dad got home, all he wanted to do was sit at the kitchen table, read the *Chronicle,* drink his beer, chuckle over *Peanuts*, and mutter "Hmmm," "Oh, yeah?" and "Is that so?" while Mom talked a blue streak about her day. Dad had retired "That's good" from his repertoire of comments, after saying it once caused Mom to bellow, "Dick, you're not even listening to me."

Dan shoved me through the back door like a prison guard roughing up his charge. "You'll never guess where I found her," he announced to our parents. "Hippie Hill!"

"Dan called me bitch!" I shouted.

Dad lowered his newspaper, his eyes smoldering.

"Joanne was with some *boy*," Dan rattled on. "I caught her before anything happened."

"What boy?" asked Mom suspiciously.

I had to think fast. "It was Paul Mathers. You know, Mom. From orchestra? He sits in the percussion section with me. He's real good on guitar, too. We were just singing."

Mom narrowed her eyes, trying to decide if she believed me.

"It was a hippie," insisted Dan. "He had long hair."

"Long hair is in *style*," I said, blushing hotly.

"Style! Look at yourself, Joanne! Anyone would mistake *you* for a hippie," said Mom. "I never knew sewing you those bell-bottoms would lead to this getup!"

Most of the kids I knew got to pick out their own clothes. Lisa Girardi had her own Macy's charge card and could choose the tiniest bikini, while my mom *made* my bathing suit. What good was a two-piece that showed only two inches of skin between the top and bottom? I would never be able to show cleavage, not in my mother's lifetime.

Dad had lost interest in the family crisis and returned to his newspaper.

Mom bent over him, her hand on her hip. "What are you going to do about this, Dick? Are you going to let *your* daughter run wild?"

"Stay out of the park, Joanne," said the newspaper.

"*What?*" Golden Gate Park was my neighborhood playground. I had visited every traveling exhibit at the de Young Museum, bought cups of flower-shaped orange crackers at the Japanese Tea Garden, and listened to free concerts at the Music

Concourse. I had been allowed to skate, ride my bike, play on the playground, and feed the ducks since I was eight, just as long as I went with someone and didn't talk to strangers. "But, Daddy! You let me go to the park even when I was a little kid."

"That was before this hippie infestation." Dad lowered his newspaper, which signaled he meant business. "You heard me, Joanne. Stay out of the park."

Dan's derisive laugh attracted Dad's attention. "And you! Tomorrow you'll change the oil in both cars."

"Dad! I got work!"

"Better get up early," said the newspaper.

Dan was terrible with cars. He couldn't even mend a flat tire without Pete's help. The last time he had tried to change the oil, it had all poured onto his face. Now who had the last laugh?

That night I lay awake, wondering how I would ever face Martin again. What did he think of me now? Would I really conform to society, as he'd predicted? Would I turn into my mother, with a telephone extension cord tail and rubber-gloved paws, and have a bald, fat husband who hid behind newspapers and thought fruit baskets were the ultimate gift?

I broke into a little fantasy then, what I called a think, about a long time in the future, when I would be old and wise and twenty-five and playing an all-Beethoven recital at Carnegie Hall, and by then Martin would be a famous folk rocker who also happened to be performing in NYC. I would find out his hotel and send him a ticket to my recital, and he would hear me play and come backstage, and we would fall into each other's arms. He would whisper in my ear, "I always knew you were special," and we would become boyfriend and girlfriend and get married and have two-point-two kids. All girls fantasized about marrying their crush, even if he happened to be Paul McCartney or, like me all my freshman year, Peter Tork of the Monkees.

# CHAPTER
# EIGHT

Mom canceled out on my parents' Thursday-night dance lesson and they ate dinner at home, so she could "keep an eye on" me. I had to have a specific reason to leave the house, and simply going to buy gum wasn't good enough. I stayed home and bided my time, knowing my mother would eventually lose interest in her assertive vigilance, as she had in the past. I practiced the piano, read, watched some TV, and got together with Rena a few times. In my room, the door slightly ajar since Mom didn't allow it closed, I lay on my bed with Snoopy curled up on my stomach, listening to records and having "thinks" about Martin. By then I had acquired my own copy of the Purple Cockroach's "Evolution! Revolution!" and nearly wore it out. I also listened to the Jefferson Airplane's *Surrealistic Pillow,* the Beatles' new *Sgt. Pepper's Lonely Hearts Club Band,* Simon and Garfunkel's *Parsley, Sage, Rosemary and Thyme,* and Judy Collins's *Wildflowers,* including "Michael from Mountains," a song that reminded me of Martin. It's about a sweet, enigmatic guy who brings a girl sweets and accompanies her on walks in streets and parks. She wants to know all about him, but she never does because "his mountains call."

The next Thursday my parents planned to go out to dinner and to their dance lesson as usual. I was past the embarrassment of Dan insulting Martin and dragging me out of the park. After my parents left the house, I forced myself to sit at the piano and at least go through the motions of practicing, and sure enough, twenty minutes later they returned home because my mother "forgot something."

After they left a second time, I slipped out of the house and ran down Masonic to catch the trolley on Haight. The white fog rolled in from the ocean, and the cold wind was damp with sea spray, typical August weather. As I climbed the steep walkway of 614 Beach Street, I could hear the Purple Cockroach rehearsing in the basement. It seemed like they never stopped. I knocked on the door, and a guy I'd never seen before answered.

When I asked for Martin, he answered, "He's in his room. Upstairs, second door on the right."

I followed the guy through the house, but just before the staircase, he abruptly walked into a candlelit, incense-scented room with mattresses and pillows covering the floor and India-print bedspreads billowing from the ceiling. It was a meditation room, occupied by three people sitting cross-legged and chanting "Om."

I mounted the staircase and reached the upper landing. Light seeped from beneath the closed second door on the right. From the room came phrases from Arlo Guthrie's *Alice's Restaurant,* along with feminine giggles and Martin's ringing laugh. Did he have lots of friends who were girls like me? Did he have an actual girlfriend and was I about to meet her? I feared the worst, imaging them in bed together, naked, doing *it.* How mortifying to interrupt that! I stood frozen in the hallway, wondering if I should leave, but after a few moments of listening to my heart pound, I decided Guthrie's long-winded story about getting arrested for littering did not seem like make-out music. I knocked quietly.

"Peace to all who enter here," said Martin.

Tentatively, I pushed open the door.

"Joni! Come in!" Martin smiled up at me and patted a spot of carpet. When I sat next to him, he said, "Morning Girl, Joni."

Morning Girl said, "May the baby Jesus shut your mouth and open your mind," whatever that meant. She didn't look much older than me, with big boobs in a flimsy top and no bra. She had full lips, and her pupils were wide disks of brown. Obviously she was stoned and so was Martin, but he seemed pretty much his usual self, while the girl looked totally wasted. She turned to Martin and said, "A maple bar is definitely a donut."

Martin shook his head. "No hole."

Arlo Guthrie said, "I wanna kill, kill. I wanna see blood and gore and guts and veins in my teeth."

"And a cinnamon roll," said Morning Girl. "That's a donut."

"No hole," said Martin. "What do you think, Joni?"

I shrugged. Being straight around stoned people was like going to a swim party on your period and having to sit on a lawn chair fully clothed while everyone else was in the pool having fun. What were Martin and Morning Girl to each other? I glanced over at his twin bed. It didn't seem big enough for two. He had a chest of drawers, a wooden crate used as a nightstand, and planks of wood set on cement blocks to serve as a bookcase. One entire wall was papered with posters of Avalon and Fillmore dances with psychedelic, bubbly printing, illustrated with biplanes, buffaloes, and Mr. Zig-Zag from the cigarette papers.

"Even donut holes are donuts," said Morning Girl.

"Donut holes are donuts with existential angst."

Morning Girl arched her neck in a silent laugh, the tip of her tongue flicking her lips. She looked so sexy I wanted to strangle her. Did I ever look sexy to Martin, or for that matter, to any guy?

Martin nudged my knee with his. "Wanna get high, Joni?"

"No."

"You told me you did."

"Not now." Not with this stupid girl babbling drivel. I had come there to have Martin to myself. I read all the titles of the books stacked on his makeshift nightstand: the Tao Te Ching, *Games People Play*, the essays of Ralph Waldo Emerson, *Siddhartha,* and *Franny and Zooey.*

"Were you homeschooled?" I asked Martin.

"Oh, is that what you call it? I thought Vivian and Max just forgot to send us to school."

I leaned into him, eager to know more. "Where are your parents now?"

"Oh, they're no place."

"Do you mean they've passed away?"

Martin released an exasperated puff of air. "Vivian is a drunk and Max is plain crazy, so I'd say that's no place." He rolled back his eyes, listening intently. From a distant room came the tiny squalls of a baby. "I hear Jericho."

"I know," Morning Girl said despondently.

This stoned girl was a *mother*? Could Martin possibly be the *father*? He'd told me he was never having kids.

Martin placed his hand on my knee. "Sorry, Joni. What were we talking about?"

"Donuts!" Morning Girl raised her arms exuberantly. "Oh, oh, I'd love a donut right now. I got the raging munchies." Then something I'd never seen happened: two round wet disks appeared at the front of her gauzy top. It took me a couple of seconds to realize what it was. She looked down at herself. "Oops. Guess Jericho's got the munchies, too. I'll go get him." She jumped up and dashed out the door.

"Does she live here?" I asked.

"Yeah. I'm kinda surprised to see you. I thought after what happened at the park your parents wouldn't let you come over anymore."

Not that they ever had. "I'm sorry my brother called you those names."

He shrugged. "Does he eat a lot of red meat?"

"He's always been like that. Trying to get me in trouble."

"That's a drag. Your brother should be your best friend."

"Not even my sister is. We're not anything alike."

"You would have to be in some ways, because the same parents raised you both."

It irked me that Martin thought he knew me better than I knew myself. I pointed toward the door. "Does the father live here?"

"What father? Oh, Jericho's? I don't think anyone knows

who that is, not even Morning Girl. We met her in Hashbury, living on the street, and she asked if we knew of a place she could crash, and Gus kinda dug her, and now he digs the whole domesticity trip of having Jericho around, so I guess she's kinda his old lady."

"She shouldn't be taking drugs if she has a baby," I blurted, more angrily than I intended.

"It's only a little weed. She's free to do what she wants. Shit, Joni, I didn't know you were so uptight and judging."

My face burned with the sting of his words. I had risked getting grounded for life to come see him and in return I'd gotten a scolding. I wasn't hip enough for him, I guess. Well, tough. I was leaving before Stupid Girl had a chance to return with her baby to expose her big, fat tit in front of me and Martin both. "That little baby's not free of cold and hunger and neglect if she's living on the street with him."

"I told you they live here. We all take care of Jericho. What are you so pissed off about?"

Still he was defending Morning Girl! I scrambled to my feet, or at least tried to. He had caught my forearm when I rose to my knees.

"Don't go away mad, Joni."

I tried to get up, and he bore down, almost as if we were wrestling. I glared at him and bit off one word at a time. "Every child has the right to know who his father is."

Astonishment washed over his face. His eyes widened and his lips parted as if to speak. From his mouth came, not words, but a kiss. It was not a music camp kiss. It was long and deep, as if he were drinking me up, and without me remembering how it happened, we ended up lying down, pressed together, and when we heard the door creak open neither of us moved apart.

"Hey, Marty," said Gus, "sit in on bass, will ya? Bread is ripped on acid, and I really wanna get 'Cold Sterling Fog' worked out tonight."

I was relieved to be facing away from the door, but Martin propped himself on an elbow to say, "Can't you see I have a guest?"

"She's a Roach fan, right? She can listen." Gus walked away as if he assumed we'd follow.

Martin looked into my face and stroked my hair. He ran his thumb over one eyebrow and held his forefinger so that my lashes flicked against it. It made me smile.

"Ah, I guess I gotta keep Gus happy. Wanna come?"

I'd rather kiss and kiss and kiss. "Sure," I said.

The basement of the house was a Victorian ballroom that had seen better days, the molding near the ceiling crumbling and the hardwood floors scuffed and gouged. Still, it made a great rehearsal studio for a rock band, housing a massive drum set, amplifiers stacked in towers, and electrical cords snaking in all directions. There they all were, the Purple Cockroach, just like they were pictured on their record sleeve. The drummer was Dave Hall, a skinny guy with a long, silky ponytail, muttonchop sideburns, and wire-rimmed granny glasses. Byron Atkins, a beefy tattooed guy, who looked more like a Hells Angel than a musician, was on rhythm guitar, and of course Gus played lead. I took a seat on the sagging sofa next to Phil Oberhofer, who went by Bread, because, I found out later, he often asked his housemates, "Got any bread?" like a live-in panhandler.

As the band tuned, I thought how this was a fantasy come true, watching Roach, up close and personal. I couldn't wait to tell Rena. As Martin flipped the strap of the bass over his head, I thought how far out it would be if he took Bread's place in the band permanently, and then I got all insecure, thinking then he'd be too important for me.

They started up, the music and feedback so loud that the walls shook. Martin played bass like a bored but obedient child, thumping out the accurate notes in a steady beat but adding nothing to them. Gus did a decent job singing lead on the verse, but when the rest of the band joined him in harmony on the chorus, they came apart and ground to a halt. After the third time, I wondered if any of them noticed that the rhythm guitar was dropping a beat.

Finally, Byron did play the correct number of beats, perhaps by accident, and they made it through the song. Bread, who had been sitting on his spine, perked up and began clapping and howling.

"What do you think?" asked Gus.

"Uh...me?" I asked.

"She knows it's crap," interjected Martin. "She plays Beethoven."

Gus glared at him. Plainly he hadn't missed how unenthusiastically Martin was participating. "We're not trying to duplicate Beethoven here."

"It's good!" I said, "but you could try substituting the submediant in the last measure of the third phrase of the chorus."

"The what?" asked Gus.

"A minor," I clarified.

"Where, again?"

"The fourth measure of the third...I mean, on the word 'cold.'"

"Oh," said Gus.

It worked out. Everyone was satisfied. During the next song, I glanced at my watch three times in five minutes, knowing it was time to go. I was hoping Martin would walk me across the street to the trolley stop, but when I stood to leave, he merely splayed two fingers and mouthed, "Peace." I spent the whole ride home in a "Cold Sterling Fog" of my own, reliving that kiss.

For one whole week the Kiss weighed heavy on my mind. It both thrilled me and scared me. I thought my next visit with Martin would be a good time to introduce Rena to him. It turned out that Roach wasn't rehearsing, so Rena didn't get to meet them. Martin was a charming host, serving his chamomile tea and some whole wheat honey cookies he'd made. Rena dominated the conversation, talking about "the theater," and Martin was responsive, telling her what he knew about Max getting his plays produced.

When it was time to leave, Martin hugged us both good-bye, which made me jealous. Whenever I went anywhere with Rena, it was obvious that guys found her more attractive than me. I worried that Martin would become more interested in her. On our trolley ride home, I discovered I had nothing to worry about.

"He knows a lot, all right," said Rena, "but he's not as cute as you think."

"What? He's the cutest guy I ever saw."

"You must be in love. "

"I'm not, either," I said, feeling the heated blush on my face.

"You *said* I'd get to meet Roach."

"Is it my fault they weren't around?"

"You *said* he'd get us high."

"All I said was he offered me grass my last visit."

Rena crossed her arms tightly and stared out the window. In a moment she turned back to me. "I'm worried about you, Joanne. I'm worried this hippie guy will get you pregnant and dash your dreams of Carnegie Hall."

"Reenie, you sound like my mother! I don't *sleep* with him."

"Eventually you'll have to. He'll force himself on you."

"Oh, he will not!"

"You're so naïve, Joanne. Haven't you read *Peyton Place*? Guys *have* to make love, while it doesn't much matter to girls one way or the other." Rena always spoke with authority about sex, when in fact she had no more experience than I. "I was crazy to go in that house with you. It's lucky we weren't both raped."

"Cripes, Rena. I can't believe how paranoid you're acting."

"What a waste. I could have been memorizing my lines."

"All six of them?" I asked.

We rode in silence the rest of the way.

The next Thursday, when I called at the house on Beach Street, Byron answered the door and told me Martin wasn't there. The following Thursday, no one answered my knock. The third week I didn't get off the trolley. I had lost my nerve.

The Summer of Love was over. Many of the runaways returned home and college kids went back to school. There were still free rock concerts in the Panhandle and plenty of hippies tucked away in low-rent apartments and partitioned Victorians, but the streets emptied out and the vibes in the Haight mellowed.

The first day of my junior year at Alamo High was so warm that most of the kids ate outside. Rena and I tried walking by the in-crowd table as if it weren't there, but then Lisa Girardi called out, "Hey, Rena, I heard you got a part at ACT."

"Yeah." Rena talked on and on about *The Crucible* until I got tired of standing there and walked off without her. All the other tables were taken up by all the other cliques. Besides the in crowd, there were a lot of other groups: the band kids, the jocks, the nerds, the weirdos, the Negroes, the Chinese, the Koreans, the Mexicans, and the Puerto Ricans.

Off in the far corner of the quad, Suyu Li sat at a small square table by herself, practicing the piano away from the keyboard, her arms flying outward, her head bobbing to the music in her mind. This was a technique I had heard Dr. Harold prescribed, but I'd never have the nerve to do it in public. I settled on an empty bench under a eucalyptus tree, unzipped my lunch pail, and tore the waxed paper off my bologna sandwich. My mother always packed my lunch in my lunch pail, even though anyone who wasn't a pariah bought lunch at the cafeteria or carried a brown bag, which they tossed away.

Rena stalked up and sat down next to me. "Thanks for waiting for me."

"I was hungry."

"There were places at their table. We could've sat with them."

"This spot is nice."

"Yeah, for lepers." Rena unrolled the top of her lunch sack and withdrew a mouthwatering, deli-style pastrami sandwich. "Ugh, squid tubes and ostrich eggs again." She dropped the sandwich back into the bag and rolled it up again.

Eventually our conversation drifted to my favorite topic, Martin's burning kiss. "It's been weeks now," I said, "and I still think about it all the time, wondering what it meant."

"Girls always know what a kiss means," Rena observed. "It

means love or at least a caring that might lead to love. Boys don't know. They kiss out of a biological urge, like a knee jerk."

"Girls have biological urges," I argued tentatively.

"Yeah, but only with guys they want to be with."

"Couldn't biological urges in boys be caused by girls they want to be with?"

Rena thought this over carefully, chewing the inside of her cheek. "Yeah, but only as a matter of coincidence."

"Oh, bummer! It's killing me not knowing when I'll see Martin again, or what he's doing."

"You know that saying, 'If you can't be with the one you love, love the one you're with'?"

"Oh! Rena! Don't tell me that!"

She laughed. "What are friends for?"

When the lunch bell rang, she tossed her whole brown-bag lunch in the garbage. I guessed that was how she stayed so skinny.

# CHAPTER
## NINE

Before my first private lesson with Dr. Harold, I attended a master class with all his other students. My mom insisted on driving me the first time, and there was some confusion getting there that Saturday morning. When we got to Dr. Harold's studio in Pacific Heights, his wife answered the door and explained that his master classes were held in the Nob Hill residence of a music patron, Mrs. H. H. Hamilton.

"The man ought to make up his mind where he does his business," Mom complained, leaning over the steering wheel as she maneuvered though traffic. No two places in San Francisco were farther than seven miles apart, but my mom acted like she had to drive through two states. "This is all nonsense, Joanne," she ranted on. "You can *walk* to Mrs. Scudder's."

I bit my lip to keep from sassing back, and when she drove up to the curb in front of Mrs. Hamiliton's mansion, I leaped out of the car before it had rolled to a stop. The piano playing had already begun by the time a maid led me into the spacious music room. Embarrassed to be late, I sat in the back. Mrs. Scudder only taught kids, and I had been one of her oldest students, but Dr. Harold's twenty-five students were high school kids, college students, older adults, and one eight-year-old prodigy.

The pianist I had walked in on was playing a brilliant Debussy prelude called "Fireworks." His hands moving up and down the keyboard were pink blurs and a flash of his gold wedding ring. How strange for me to be a part of a class with a *married* person in it. It made me feel grown-up.

After the student finished playing and everyone clapped, Dr. Harold rose from his seat at the front of the room to lead a discussion. He was a lean man with a trimmed black beard, horn-rimmed glasses, and wavy hair. His movements were energetic and graceful. Already I loved watching him and listening to him talk.

Although I couldn't think of a thing wrong with the dazzling performance I had just heard, Dr. Harold and his students had plenty of comments. They said the pianist had rushed in the middle section, his hands were not playing exactly together at times, and he needed to bring out the melody in the fiery section of cross-hand movements.

Suyu played next, the fourth and most difficult Chopin ballade, with an opening melody so rich and warm, I felt like a giant Hershey kiss melting in my chair. I fell into a rapture, not only enjoying her beautiful playing, but thinking that under Dr. Harold's guidance and with lots of hard work, I would someday play that well.

The critiques that ensued after Suyu's performance made me fume. Why were these snotty people picking apart such wonderful playing? I shifted in my seat, anxious to be a part of the discussion and defend Suyu.

Finally I raised my hand and blurted, "I thought it was really good!" My boisterous acclamation echoed in the sonorous room.

Everyone turned and looked at me. No one agreed or disagreed. I slid down on my spine, thinking my stupid, superficial comment had revealed my ignorance.

Dr. Harold pressed his hands together and rested his chin on his fingertips. "Could you tell us what in particular was good?"

"Hmm...just everything. The melody was as smooth and velvety as chocolate icing."

Everyone laughed, and suddenly I was too warm in my sweater. Why couldn't I learn to keep quiet?

"This is Joanne Donnelly, the newest member of our family," said Dr. Harold. "Please stand, Joanne."

I rose slowly from my seat, flushing even more. Applause and smiles erupted. I took a bow. It felt awkward to bow for doing nothing. Then I realized it was for something: acceptance, and for that I felt relieved and grateful.

Next, the little kid rattled off the first movement of a Mozart sonata with his lightning-fast fingers. This elicited a lengthy discussion about how a pianist projected expression in his playing. Didn't expression just happen? Wasn't that, in fact, the easiest aspect of playing?

Finally Dr. Harold ended the formal part of the gathering with announcements. As usual, his students would be performing a holiday recital at the Palace of Fine Arts to benefit the San Francisco Symphony. "I'll leave the sign-up sheet here on this chair. Be sure to include the title of your piece."

I almost knocked a few people over getting second in line for the sign-up sheet. After I wrote my name and Beethoven's "*Pathétique*" sonata behind it, I noticed Dr. Harold watching me, his lower lip curled into his mouth and his teeth biting down thoughtfully. I thought he was going to say something to me about signing up, but then the moment passed, and I forgot about it. I couldn't wait to get home to brag to my mom that I would be performing at the Palace of Fine Arts.

Dr. Harold was married to another Dr. Harold, a child psychiatrist. Students taking their piano lessons in Dr. Harold's studio could often hear children shrieking on the other side of the wall, just as the patients of his wife could hear piano playing while they were in therapy. The two Dr. Harolds shared their waiting room, which was packed with toys. Waiting for my first lesson, I was more excited than nervous. I yearned to get down on my knees and play with the little kitchen set along with the little kids.

At last Dr. Harold invited me into his studio and adjusted his bench to the precisely right height for me. I handed him my music, took my place at his ebony Steinway grand, and pounced on the opening chords of my Beethoven sonata. I made it to the fifth measure before he stopped me to lecture on arm weight and relaxation. He instructed me to play a C major scale to demonstrate what he meant. On each note I was to drop my wrist, which would lead my arm weight to the key bed.

Every time I tried to do this, he said, "No, no."

Next he told me to play the C scale in contrary motion, and showed me how to stretch my thumb under my hand, then whip my hand over the thumb when going in the opposite direction.

I tried to follow his instructions, and he said, "No, no."

He came behind me, pressed down my shoulders, told me how tension was gathering there, which obstructed a warm, singing tone. The minutes of my precious hour with Dr. Harold ticked by. I glanced forlornly at my Beethoven sonata, discarded on his chair. Would we ever get back to it?

No. Besides the Beethoven, he assigned me a Bach prelude and fugue, a Chopin nocturne, and Debussy's *"Claire de lune,"* which I had played in the sixth grade. "But mostly I want to you concentrate on the C scale, Joanne," he said in the last minutes of my lesson. "You'll be able to apply these techniques to your pieces once you understand them in playing the scale."

I nodded and smiled wanly, feeling spasms at the corners of my mouth. It wasn't until I got home and was sitting at the kitchen table with my parents that I allowed my disappointment to burst forth in tears. "Dr. Harold treated me like a beginner. He made me start all over with the C major scale!"

"You know a lot more than that!" said Mom. "Mrs. Scudder told me you knew *all* your scales years ago. He thinks if he starts you over he can make more money off us!"

"No, Mom. He's teaching me technique. Of all his students, I'm the worst one!"

"He told you you could play Beethoven at the Palace of Fine Arts. Now, at the Palace of Fine Arts, you're going to play the C scale?" One side of Mom's nose wrinkled up and her mouth hung open.

I remembered then that Dr. Harold had not given me

permission to play; I had merely signed up. Recalling the look on his face when I had done so, I gasped for breath in the middle of a jagged sob.

Dad couldn't bear to hear his girls cry. It always made him start yelling. He folded his newspaper to say, "Quit your blubbering, Joanne. And stop this damn piano nonsense. It takes talent, and no one in this family has got any talent."

"Don't tell her that, Dick!" exclaimed Mom.

"Someone's got to. Take up typing, Joanne, so you can get a good job like your smart sister."

I should have known better than to confide in my parents. They never understood anything about me. I ran upstairs, threw myself facedown on my bed, and muffled my sobs in Snoopy's fur. My fantasy life had just had a head-on collision with reality, and I thought I'd die of the injuries. I could no longer gloss over the hard parts and speed through the easy parts and shine on Dr. Harold the way I had Mrs. Scudder. I was going to have to take his instruction, apply it to my playing, bend to his will. The whole time he was talking, I'd kept thinking, This is stupid, a waste of time. When am I going to get to play my Beethoven? I'd understood practically nothing of my first lesson, and not once had Dr. Harold said anything good about my playing. It hurt me to think that I was going to have to do everything his way. It hurt more to doubt that I actually could.

All the rest of the week, I read and reread Dr. Harold's notes in my assignment book and practiced the C major scale the way he'd told me to. One afternoon, I was startled to find Dan standing in the foyer near the front door, leering at me.

"Dwight could do better than that."

Dwight was Pete's Mongoloid brother. I leaped from the bench, and all my frustrations came out in a windmill of fisticuffs thumping soundly on Dan's back. He covered his head with his arms, laughing and shouting, "Mom! Mom!" until she came in from the kitchen with a wooden spoon in her hand. "What are you doing home, Dan? I thought you had class."

"Couldn't find a parking place so I just came home."

"Take the streetcar if there's no parking."

Dan loped off to his room without answering her. I'd overheard him tell Pete that he cut class a lot.

On another afternoon, I dashed home from school, anxious to practice, only to hear Mom's bridge group in the den, cackling and talking all at once. I couldn't just play the dumb C scale with all of them in earshot, so I worked on Beethoven. Out of the corner of my eye, I was startled to see Maxine Fulmer seated on the sofa. Apparently Mom's bridge group were on their bundt cake break.

"Oh, am I distracting you, Joanne? I just love to listen to you play."

"Thank you, Mrs. Fulmer."

"Maxine, honey, remember? And how is that beautiful sister of yours doing?"

"Okay, I guess. We don't see her that much."

"It's a shame she cut her education so short. Your mother was so proud of her for getting into Cal."

"Really? She never told Denise."

"Your mother may not always show it, but she's proud of you kids."

Neither of my parents had gone to college, but ever since we were little kids, they'd told us we would be attending nearby San Francisco State College.

"I adore being back in school again," continued Maxine. "I've changed my major to a new offering—women's studies. It's just fascinating, and it gives Quentin and me so much to talk about."

"How's he doing?"

She shrugged and gave a pert smile. "Trying to find himself. One day he's a poet, the next a politician. He's young, you know, but he's such good company."

When the bridge party was over, Thelma Newman and Leona Dunbar loitered in the kitchen to help Mom clean up, I figured just so they could gossip about Maxine. I resorted to my C major scale, playing *pianissimo* so I could eavesdrop.

"*Women's studies*?" shrieked Mrs. Newman. "What *is* that?"

"What's there to study about cleaning and cooking that we don't already know?" asked Mom.

"And she's shacked up with that *boy*," said Mrs. Dunbar. "It's one thing to be discreet, but she's simply brazen about it."

"Apparently he's living off her, and they're both living off her alimony," said Mrs. Newman. "I thought women's libbers wanted to be independent of men!"

"Considering what that son of a gun Ronald Fulmer put her through, Maxine has earned every penny of that alimony," said Mom.

Hooray! I was glad at least one of those clucking hens had stuck up for Maxine, and I was proud it was my mom.


On Saturday, Mom plopped four quarters in my hand and sent me to pick up Dad's two pairs of suit pants at Li's Laundry and Dry Cleaners. I waited until late afternoon, hoping Suyu would be gone by then, because I didn't want to answer any embarrassing questions about my first lesson with Dr. Harold.

At twenty to five, Mom called, "Joanne! Haven't you gone to the cleaners yet? Do you expect your father to go to work Monday morning in his undershorts?"

I ran all the way to Stanyan Street. Suyu was perched on her stool behind the register, a tablet on her knee and a thick calculus textbook open on the counter.

She looked up and said, "Oh, hi, Joanne." She leaped off her stool, retrieved my father's pants from the "D" clothes rack, and hung them on the hook next to the cash register. "How'd your first lesson go?"

"Okay, I guess," I said in a dejected tone.

"The C major scale, eh? Don't worry. That's what everyone gets assigned their first lesson."

"I don't know what he's talking about," I admitted.

"It's something you'll feel when it's right, and once you have it, you have it. Here, I'll show you." She lifted a section of the counter, which was hinged, but I hesitated. In all the years I'd been coming to Li's, I'd never been on the opposite side of the counter, which seemed forbidden territory. "Come on," urged Suyu. "It's okay."

I stepped forward, and she lowered the counter. She extended her forearm. "Now, this is the piano. Sink the weight of your arm into it." I set my hand on her arm. Quickly she lowered her arm, leaving my hand in midair.

"Ah! You see? You are holding your arm up by your shoulder. Sink it into the piano. Try again." She raised her forearm again, and this time I pressed down on it. "No, you are pushing! Here, you be the piano this time."

Suyu was a tiny person, and it was surprising to me how heavy her thin arm felt on my forearm. "Take away your arm," she said, and when I did, her arm swung to her side. She smiled. "You see? My arm fell because you were holding all of its weight. Now you try."

When we changed positions, Suyu used the fingers of her other hand to probe the muscle in my shoulder. "Let go, here! Let go...let go!"

I felt it! Suyu swung her arm away and my arm dropped!

I thanked Suyu over and over. I ducked under the counter, grabbed my father's pants off the hook, and darted out of the shop. Suyu locked the door behind me and turned the sign from OPEN to CLOSED. It wasn't until I reached the corner of Stanyan and Frederick that I realized I was still clutching the four quarters in my hand. I could give them to Suyu at school on Monday, but meanwhile her cash register would come up a dollar short. I felt terrible about that, but I was ecstatic, too. Finally, I understood arm weight!

# CHAPTER
## TEN

I hated my birthdays. They were supposed to be so special, but I was almost always disappointed. The previous year I had begged and begged my mom to let me have a party, and finally she'd allowed me to invite five girls for a sleepover. I chose Rena, Lisa Girardi, and three of the other in-crowd girls. Lisa ate my food, listened to a couple of records, then began to pace around the living room, picking up things and setting them down. A little after ten, she announced she wanted to go home, so all the other girls did, too. Except Rena, of course. It ended up being just me and her sitting around scarfing Fritos and wondering what had gone wrong.

With my sixteenth birthday only a week away, I tried not to think about it. What if no one remembered? Rena was so busy juggling *Crucible* rehearsals and school, she couldn't think of much else. Mom would go the whole route, of course, make me a special dinner and sew something I didn't want to wear. The whole birthday trip was just a bummer.

It actually turned out to be pretty neat. Rena had play practice, of course, but she made me a beautiful belt out of suede with a row of little mirrors she sewed on. Denise and Jerry came over and Mom made me my favorite dinner, chicken fricassee with dumplings, and German chocolate cake. The big surprise was that she sewed me a cool Nehru jacket out of black-and-red paisley, with black frog closures and a red lining. No other girl at school would have anything like it.

Dad gave me a patch of Schroeder playing the piano with the words I LOVE BEETHOVEN embossed around the circumference to sew on the back pocket of my jeans. It was extra-special, because he usually left the gift-buying to Mom. Of course Dan didn't take off work to be at my birthday dinner, but he set on the kitchen table a tiny yellow glass vase with paper flowers in it, something the tourists bought at the Cannery, but I really liked it.

Denise and Jerry presented me with recordings of the complete Beethoven sonatas, twelve LPs, packed in four flat cardboard boxes, which was more than they could afford. Jerry signed their card "to Beethoven from Beethoven," making him probably the coolest brother-in-law ever. He had a crease across the pocket of his white Oxford shirt, a clue that Denise's ironing had become careless. She looked tired, as if her shoulders could hardly bear the weight of her husband's arm draped casually over them. She seemed much older than she had before her wedding, a few short months ago. After they left, I was relieved my birthday was over. I had been fifteen long enough.

Thursday evening, the following week, I was practicing Beethoven after dinner, having progressed far beyond the C scale. Dr. Harold had scheduled me to play my sonata in master class the last week of November, and that gave me the incentive to work even harder. The phone rang, and I didn't want to answer it. After the fourth ring my mother yelled in from the den, where she was sitting with my dad watching *Peyton Place*.

"Get that, Joanne! It's probably Rena."

I picked up the phone. "Hello?"

"Joni! What's happening?"

"Hi-ay" came out on two pitches, my surprise apparent.

Only one person in the whole world called me Joni. Had Martin found my number in the phone book? I wasn't sure he even knew or remembered my last name.

"Can I see you?" he asked.

I glanced toward the den. "Now?"

"Now is always the best time."

Beach Street was far, far away, and it was almost bedtime. "I can't."

"I'm here in Hashbury. I came to visit you."

"Where?" I asked hopefully.

"In the phone booth at Masonic and Haight. We can meet at the Tangerine Kangaroo."

"It's late."

"In front of your house, then. I'll start walking there right now."

"Okay." I hung up.

Mom called, "Who was it?"

"Rena." I dashed upstairs to grab a textbook, then ran down again. I poked my head into the den. "She forgot her chemistry book in her locker so I'm loaning her mine." I sprinted toward the front door.

"She's the one who needs it," said Mom. "She's the one who can come get it."

I slammed the door on my mother's words, then sped down the porch steps, through the gate, down the outside steps to the street, and fell into a warm, hard hug behind the retaining wall, my chemistry book crashing to the sidewalk.

"Missed you, lady," Martin whispered in my ear. He let go just enough to hold my face in his hands. "Why did you stop coming over? Did I do something?"

"I did come over, but Byron said you weren't home, and then another time—well, it's harder now. I've got school, and you never want to plan anything, so—"

His concerned look broke into a wide grin. "We can plan something!" He clasped my hands and playfully swung our arms between us. "Let's spend Saturday together, the whole day!"

"Can't. I have master class."

"Can't you ditch, like, one time?"

"No! It's the best time of my whole week—well, second best. Best is my piano lesson. I love my new teacher!"

"And I love you!" He bounced on the balls of his feet. "Come play with me, Joni, on Saturday!"

The word "love" got a lot of use. I'm not saying it was over-used; I'm not sure that's possible, but that one little word had so many shades of meaning that its four little letters needed to explode into about fifty new words to express them all. "Oh, Martin, you love everything. You love this city, you love this tree, you love this chemistry book." I picked it up and held it up to him. "Here, kiss it."

He did, and then he kissed me, softly, sweetly, deeply. His hand slid up my waist to cup my breast, and I impulsively hooked my elbow over his wrist and pushed it away. I didn't know where that had hand been, how many girls' bodies it had roamed over since it had last touched mine. I was going to be someone special to him or nothing at all.

"Oh, Joni, you feel so good," he moaned, holding me tighter. "I need you, girl."

Then what had taken him so long to come around? "We can do something on Saturday after my master class. It's on Nob Hill."

"Right next to Chinatown. Let's have lunch there." He rubbed his hands together. "Dim sum, duck with plum sauce, eels in squid ink!"

I knew he was kidding about the last dish. "What about 'Simplify, simplify, simplify'?"

"Gotta splurge sometimes."

A flood of light appeared above our retaining wall. It meant Mom had turned on the front porch light and was coming to look for me. "Meet you at noon at the Dragon's Gate," I whispered to Martin, then kissed him on the ear. Toward the house, I shouted, "Coming, Mom!"

Martin peeked above the retaining wall, beneath the shrub-bery. "Nice digs," he said. I thought I might have detected a slight longing in his tone.

"Go!" I gave him a shove up the hill toward Masonic. I ran up the steps and met my mom just inside the gate.

"Joanne, you still have your chemistry book in your hand."

I looked down at it. "Oh, yeah. Rena didn't really want it. She just needed to tell me something."

"And she couldn't do it over the phone? What about?"

"Uh, it was about—"

"Never mind." Mom gave me a hurt, disgusted look, and I felt guilty. How could I confide in her? She wouldn't allow half the stuff I did. I put my arm around her waist as we went up the steep porch steps, which made her puff.

"Don't worry so much, Mom. I'm not as bad as you think."

I was worse.

As I scurried down California Street, past Grace Cathedral, the balls of my feet burned in a way that warned me blisters were forming. In the bottom of my right shoe were four folded one-dollar bills, which I hoped would be enough for my lunch. I was wearing patent leather pumps; nylons; a brown tweed suit Mom had tailored, with a skirt that hit the middle of my knee; and a ruffled butterscotch blouse. Master class had run over a half hour, and I didn't realize how long it would take me to get down Nob Hill to Chinatown.

After Mom had driven me to the first master class, I'd used public transportation. I had told her a half-truth, that I was having lunch in Chinatown with a group of kids from Dr. Harold's studio, and then I was going to the main library in Civic Center to work on a term paper for history.

"Dad and I are going to Uncle Herb and Aunt Meg's for dinner," she had told me. "There's a TV dinner for you in the freezer. Get home before dark. I'm going to call to check on you." She had hooked a dark-penciled eyebrow at me to indicate she meant business, but I knew she was bluffing. My dad's brother and his wife lived in San Jose, about an hour away, which was long-distance, and my mom never made an unnecessary expensive phone call. This dinner had no doubt been arranged by Aunt Meg and Mom exchanging little note cards, which only cost a five-cent stamp to send. It would be hard to know when my parents would be home. If Dad and Uncle Herb were getting along, my parents would stay and play bridge after dinner; if they weren't, my parents would be home early.

Nearly an hour late to meet Martin, I braced myself for utter disappointment. As I approached the stone arch of Dragon's Gate, there was Martin panhandling, collecting the price of his lunch.

"I'm late," I said, puffing, reaching for a hug.

"Are you?" Martin did not wear a watch. "There's so much to see around here, I didn't even notice." He looked me up and down. "You're so . . . dressed up."

What he meant was *straight*. "Yeah, for master class."

"Are you comfortable?"

I shook my head and offered him a forlorn look. He laughed, took my hand, and led me to the Red Lion, where we gorged ourselves on abundant, cheap Chinese food. He told me about his latest adventure, how he had hiked up Mount Tamalpais. "What's been happening with you, Joni?"

I sighed. "Mostly doing battle with Beethoven."

"I would never play music if it meant going to war."

I tried to pinch another pot sticker with the chopsticks Martin had just taught me to use, and it fell back onto the plate. "I know you spend hours on the guitar, working out a new song."

"Only if I want to. As soon as I'm tired of it, I put it down."

I chased the pot sticker around with my sticks. "You didn't want to play bass with Roach that time. I could tell."

"Oh, well, that's different. I was doing Gus a favor."

"How's the Roach album coming along?"

He frowned. "Slow, but Gus signed a contract with Bill Graham to play three weekends at the Fillmore in the spring."

"Oh! Oh! Could you sneak me in?"

"Sure."

"Really? And Rena, too?"

"Rena? That theater type you brought over that one time?"

"Rena isn't a type. She's my best friend."

"All theater people are the same. Self-centered egomaniacs."

Clearly my two favorite people in the whole world were not impressed with each other. It made me sad. "Wow, I didn't know you were so uptight and judging."

He cocked his head and smiled wryly. "Sor-ree." He picked up the pot sticker I'd been pursuing and popped it into my mouth. "You have to sneak in, huh?"

"Age doesn't matter," I said, quoting him again. "I had a birthday last week."

"Happy birthday. Which one?"

I swallowed the pot sticker and grinned.

"I have to sneak into the Fillmore, too," he admitted. "It's not that hard."

This good news made me laugh: "I thought you were way over eighteen!"

"Nope, the government's going to let me live a few more months."

The draft. It hovered like the black angel of death in the soul of every American boy. "I'm sixteen," I announced.

"Sweet sixteen and...kissed. I know for a fact you've been kissed." He leaned over the table and kissed me lightly right then. I worried about my breath, but he said, "Mmm, ginger!" Kiss. "And garlic!" Kiss. "And soy sauce! You're delicious."

The waiter set the bill on a little tray next to Martin. I took my four sweaty dollar bills out of my shoe and set them on top, and Martin added some change, leaving a small tip.

From Chinatown, we walked through North Beach, past the marina. "I wanted to take you to Muir Woods today," said Martin, "but we really need all day for that."

"Sorry," I said.

"I know where we can go." We crossed the Golden Gate Bridge, and when I stuck my thumb out at Martin's direction, I imagined the atom bomb dropping over us, everything blowing away, including myself and Martin, in a fierce, hot mushroom cloud.

A maroon luxury sedan pulled over to pick us up. Inside was a friendly couple, about my parents' age, from Kansas, who asked us all kinds of funny questions about being hippies as we drove the fifteen miles to Tiburon. From there, Martin and I took the ferry to Angel Island. My whole life, I had looked across the San Francisco Bay beyond Alcatraz, to the green-and-brown hump of Angel Island, but I had never set foot on it. I knew it had once been an immigration station mostly for Orientals, the West Coast's version of Ellis Island, but now the few rickety buildings weren't used, and the island had mostly reverted to its natural state. No cars were allowed, so visitors traveled along the rough asphalt of its circumference on foot, bikes, and roller skates. Martin wanted to walk around the perimeter of the island, but by then I had blisters on my soles, heels, and toes.

Martin looked down at his sturdy boots and my pumps. "Why are you wearing those?"

"I told you. I had to be dressed up for master class."

He shook his head. "Not worth it. There should be no such thing as shoes you can't walk in."

I looked around at the other visitors and noticed I was the only one in a suit, nylons, and heels, except for a few old ladies. Walking the wooded dirt trails, I carried my shoes. It wasn't long before I had runs in my stockings, but I was too inhibited to lift my skirt and unhook the garters in front of Martin. Besides, it was cold.

On a sandy beach, we sat huddled together, talking and sharing a joint. It burned my throat and didn't have much effect. It was one of those great mysteries of life I had anticipated, only to feel let down when I unlocked it. At least I would be able to tell Rena and to hold in my own brain the thought, I smoked pot! The wind commanded Martin's hair to spiral and dance. I could have watched it forever.

We lay on the beach and kissed, and when the touching got too intense, I pushed him away. He sat up, hooked his arms over his knees, and stared out across the bay. "You're sure pure."

"I like to take things slow."

"You know I love you," he said, still not looking at me.

"And Susie and Kathy and Judy and Cindy and Morning Girl."

He got up in a huff and strode across the sand. I loved watching him walk in his lanky, loose-jointed way. He was a beautiful boy, even if he could never be mine.

I wondered if he was going to leave me there, stranded on the chilly beach without even the price of the ferry ride, but soon he circled back and pulled me to my feet and into his embrace. "I can't make you any promises, Joni, but for now, there's just you. Do you believe me when I tell you that?"

"I guess."

"What do you mean you guess?" But he was laughing, and we had made it through our first fight.

The trouble with hitchhiking was that it wasn't reliable, especially if you had to sneak back into your house before your parents got home. It was dusk when Martin and I returned to Tiburon by ferry, and then we stood on the road outside town in the dark with our thumbs sticking out for a couple of hours. I fervently hoped Dad and Uncle Herb were getting along and the after-dinner bridge game was on. I was shivering and depressed, my stomach rumbling from hunger.

"You've got to smile if you expect someone to pick us up," said Martin.

"I'm scared I won't ever get home tonight."

"I know what." He hid behind a bush, and when a car stopped with two men in it and I opened the door to the backseat, Martin leaped in beside me. On the San Francisco side of the Golden Gate Bridge, we got out on Lincoln Avenue. Martin and I hugged good-bye, and we took public transportation our separate ways. When I got off the trolley at Haight Street, I slipped off my shoes again and ran all the way home.

It was after nine, and our house was dark. I had made it! Using the key under the fourth flowerpot, I let myself in the back door and dashed through the house, eager to get out of my suit and into the shower before my parents returned. I bounded up the stairs and pushed open my bedroom door.

In the darkness, a man talked in a gravelly voice while a woman gently sobbed. My heart nearly exploded out of my chest.

# CHAPTER
# ELEVEN

It was Rod McKuen, murmuring his sad breakup poetry on an LP recording of *Stanyan Street and Other Sorrows*. I didn't have to turn on the light to know who was sniffling his accompaniment, but I did anyway.

"You scared the crap out of me, Denise."

"Sorry. I just came here for a little rest." She was flung on her little girl's bed with bloodshot eyes and a nose red from crying. "Where've you been?"

"At the movies with Rena," I lied. "Don't tell Mom."

"Why? What did you see?"

I dropped my chin, striving for a guilty look. "*You Only Live Twice*."

"Shame on you, Joanne!" she said in her big-sister scolding voice. "Those James Bond movies are for adults!"

"Don't tell Mom. What's the matter?"

"Oh, nothing."

"Something is."

"I loved playing house when I was little. I thought all I needed was my very own stove and refrigerator to be set for life." Denise squinted and sniffed. "You smell like marijuana."

I held the sleeve of my jacket under my nose and inhaled ocean, soy sauce, patchouli, Martin, and pot. "Yeah. This tweedy stuff traps odors, and the whole neighborhood smells of it."

Denise frowned. "The whole Bay Area."

Rod McKuen had stopped moaning in his dejected, raspy voice. I didn't much care for him, but his poetry books and records sold millions. It made me think there must be a lot of brokenhearted people who liked to lie in the dark crying. The needle on the turntable floated back and forth in the center of the record. I lifted the arm, hooked it in place, and shut off the record player.

"I miss school," said Denise. "But Gerald says a degree in art history is pointless. All I could do with it is be a docent in a museum, and those jobs are for men. He told me, 'You don't want to take a job away from a man who needs it to feed his family.'"

"That's stupid! You're the one feeding your family now."

"I hate my job!" said Denise in a little squeaky voice. "I hate Mr. Marlowe! I correct his grammar in the letters he dictates to me, and then he changes it back. 'Dear Sir: A representative from Manning Corporation will meet with you and *I*.'"

"That's terrible! Everyone who's been to the seventh grade knows objective-case pronouns follow prepositions."

"Not Mr. Marlowe, and he's the president of a whole advertising agency! So then I have to stay at the office late, sneak the letter from outgoing mail, and retype it *again* to correct it."

I batted the air. "Why bother?"

"Because everyone just assumes if there's a mistake in a letter, it's the dumb secretary's fault."

Miss Perfect couldn't allow that. I went into the bathroom to brush my teeth, wash my face, and change. I tugged off my panty girdle and massaged the red, indented lines it left on my body before slipping into my comfy flannel pajamas. I returned to the bedroom and began hanging up my suit.

"Where is everybody?" asked Denise, propped on an elbow.

"Mom and Dad are at Uncle Herb's and Dan's at work. Does Jerry know you're here?"

"No. He had some psychology seminar thing all day. I thought I'd come over here for a few hours' visit, but now I guess I'll spend the night."

"Won't he wonder where you are when he comes home and finds you're gone?"

"I don't care. I thought being married would be a lot better. More comforting."

I blurted, "Don't you like doing *it*?"

Denise blushed. After a moment, she said, "Yes, I do. It's nice. At least, I liked it at first, but then Gerald started complaining about my sexual performance. He says I have clitoral orgasms, not mature vaginal orgasms, which means I'm frigid. But it's not my fault. It may take me years of psychoanalysis to resolve my sexual frustration. He says probably I was sexually abused as a child and don't remember it."

I was staring at her so hard I could feel my eye sockets straining to contain my eyeballs. "You were never abused. I'd know. I've been with you night and day our whole lives."

"Well, that's what Gerald says."

"Denise, this may come as a shock. Jerry doesn't know everything."

Denise huffed indignantly. "I shouldn't be telling you any of this. It just came pouring out. I don't have anybody to talk to."

"Mom would freak out if you said any of this stuff to her. I'll bet she and Daddy did it only three times."

"Joanne, that's not true. Don't you ever hear them in the night?"

"Our *parents* have sex? Still? That the grossest thing I've ever heard!"

"Why would they give it up? They seem a lot better at it than Jerry and I."

"You should try talking to Maxine."

"Who's that?"

"Mrs. Fulmer."

"Oh, her." Denise wrinkled her nose.

"She knows a lot! She's studying women at the university. And she's the only one of Mom's friends who talks to me like I'm a real person."

"She couldn't know more about it than Gerald. He's an expert.

His dissertation is on Freud and female genital sexuality." She raised her hand and rubbed her thumb over her wedding ring. "I also thought this would be protection."

"Protection?"

"From men grabbing at me. Just about every date I ever went on turned into a wrestling match. I was just so sick of it I thought, Well, I'll get married and be done with it, but no, nearly every day Mr. Marlowe needs a file out of the 'P' drawer."

"Huh?"

"It's right in the middle of the filing cabinet. I have to bend over to pull it out, and when I do, he wanders behind me and rubs up against me. 'Pardon, Denise,' he says, like it's an accident. Sometimes I think I even feel his hands on my . . . on me. And when I take shorthand, he stands behind me and *breathes*."

"He breathes?"

"Real heavy. I don't know what he's doing back there, sniffing my hair, looking down my blouse." Denise shuddered.

"Can't you complain to someone?"

"Who, the boss? He's the boss!"

The phone rang. I went into the hallway to answer it.

"Joanne? Is Denise there?" Jerry was obviously mad or he would have called me Beethoven.

"Yeah. She just came over for a little visit."

"What am I supposed to do for dinner? I'm starving!"

Every night my dad came home to my mother in her apron and fresh lipstick, fixing his dinner, but it made me mad that Jerry expected the same from Denise when she also had to work for that awful Mr. Marlowe. "Oh, make yourself a PB and J, Jerry *Whiner*field. What are you, helpless?"

"Gerald's dinner!" Denise shrieked, and dashed to the phone. She snatched the receiver from me and said, "Oh, honey, I'm so sorry! I forgot all about . . . Yes, I know you expect steak and mashed potatoes on Saturday . . . Darling, yes. I'll make it up to you. I'll fry a chicken tomorrow." As Denise stood on one bare foot, then the other, listening to her raging husband, I crept into bed and pulled the covers over my head.

*   *   *

Dad could cook one thing, and that was Sunday-morning waffles. He was artful, stuffing them with chopped apples, cinnamon, and raisins before cooking, or heaping them with bananas and hazelnuts afterward.

As Mom, Denise, and I sat at the kitchen table waiting for our waffles to be served, Mom scolded Denise for deserting Jerry overnight. "Don't come home crying to us at the least provocation. You made your bed, now sleep in it."

Dad commanded the waffle iron, wearing his chef apron with the picture of the *Peanuts* Snoopy holding his dish in his mouth above SUPPERTIME in bright red letters, while our Snoopy wove between his legs. This morning Dad had outdone himself by cooking blueberries to a gooey syrup on the inside of the waffles and nestling plump strawberries in whipped cream on top.

The moment he proudly set the steaming plates before us, there came two sharp raps on the back door. Jerry let himself in and stood bleary-eyed and rumpled at the entrance to the kitchen.

"Good morning, Jerry!" exclaimed Mom. "Just in time for waffles."

"No, thank you," he said stiffly. "I've got lots to do today. Ready, Denise?"

Denise frowned and looked down at her full plate.

I made a face at him. "Sit down and have some waffles, Jerry. You know you want to."

He smirked back at my taunting. "They do look awfully good."

Mom pulled out Dan's chair and patted the seat. "Sit, darling. You're in for a treat. Dick's waffles are outstanding."

Jerry grinned and leaped into the chair. The crackling tension in the room dissipated, replaced by homey Sunday-morning "Mmms" between bites of blueberry waffles.

"I've got papers to write and papers to correct," said Jerry around an overstuffed mouth. "It's not like I have it easy like you, Denise, with just a five-day-a-week job."

Denise's fork halted midway between her plate and mouth, a stricken look on her face.

"Did you hear that, Denise?" I said. "Old Jerry boy is giving you the whole day off. You won't have to fry that chicken after all. Where you taking her to dinner, Jer, huh? Huh?"

Jerry pointed his knife at me. "You know what I meant, Beethoven. I'm talking about *paid* work."

"Denise knows a woman's work is never done," said Mom cheerfully.

"I thought Lincoln freed the slaves," I said. "Oh, wait a minute. Those were Negroes."

Denise snorted into her coffee, stifling a laugh, while Jerry's eyes slid in my direction. I gave him a fake smile.

"*Okay.* We can go to that little Afghani restaurant on Shattuck, Denise. The food's good and it's cheap."

"I'll fry the chicken, Gerald. No problem."

"No, I want to take you out." He reached across the table and gave her hand a squeeze. Their eyes met. "We haven't had any time together this whole weekend."

Dad went "Hmph," and scraped his chair across the floor to reach for the *Chronicle*.

After Jerry and Denise left, Mom remarked, "I don't know where you get such notions, Joanne."

"What notions?"

"You know. That women's libbers' lip service. You shouldn't interfere in your sister's marriage." Mom bent to clear the table.

"Oh, Mommy, Jerry likes it when I joke around with him. He's like the brother I never had."

"You have a brother," said the newspaper.

"I mean one who's nice to me."

"What got into Denise to come running home, Mother?" asked the newspaper. "Did you ever get to the bottom of it?"

"I know exactly what's going on with Denise," said Mom. "Remember, Dick, early on in our marriage, why I went running home to my mother?"

"No," said the newspaper.

Mom set a pile of dirty dishes on the counter and pressed one rubber-gloved finger against her chin. "I'll just bet we're about to become grandparents. If it's a boy, I wonder if it will look like you, Dick."

"What, Mom? You think the kid is going to be a newspaper?"

# CHAPTER
# TWELVE

My piano lesson was nearly over. I turned my wrist to glance at my watch, trying to build up the courage to break the news to Dr. Harold.

"You seem distracted, Joanne," he said as he made his final notes in my assignment book.

"Um...I need to tell you something. I'll have to miss master class this Saturday."

"You know I expect all my students to be there for one another every time. What's the reason?"

"Uh...it's kind of a special event, a family thing."

"A birthday?"

"No."

"A wedding?"

"No."

Dr. Harold laughed and drew his fingers through his wavy black hair. "Why is this turning into a guessing game? Just tell me, Joanne."

I knew I couldn't play games with Dr. Harold the way I did with my mother and maintain his respect. "I'm going to the Stop the Draft march," I blurted.

"With your *family*?" he exclaimed incredulously. He had met my mother.

"No. My mom doesn't know. She wouldn't let me. Don't tell on me."

"Hmm...it sounds dangerous. Do you understand what you're getting into?"

I shrugged. I didn't really know much about it. Martin had said he was going to Berkeley to protest the war and had invited me along.

Dr. Harold reached for the *Chronicle* and gestured toward the lead article. "The demonstrators are planning to march on the army induction center and forcibly shut it down for a week. The mayor of Oakland won't grant the permit for the march, so everyone who participates is breaking the law."

"Martin Luther King sometimes marches without a permit."

"And he's sometimes met with violence." Dr. Harold tapped the newspaper with the back of his hand. "These demonstrators are trying to stop the war machine of the United States of America, and there's going to be trouble." I knew Dr. Harold was opposed to the war because he said "war machine" instead of just "war," and I'd seen the peace-sign bumper sticker on his Citroen. "The Oakland chief of police vows to stop the demonstrators by any means, even calling out the National Guard. Those guys have rifles."

That made me think of the picture in my world history textbook of Bloody Sunday in 1905, when workers marched on the czar's winter palace and his army fired into the crowd, killing hundreds. "So? This isn't Russia. They won't shoot anybody just for walking around."

"Don't be too sure of that. I participated in Vietnam Day last year about this time, and they threw tear gas into the crowd. My eyes burned for a month. Wait a minute. My God, that was *two* years ago. Consensus war, my ass!"

Dr. Harold was the type of adult who swore in front of kids and didn't apologize for it. He was pacing the room with his quick, energetic stride. My lesson had gone over five minutes, and he kept strict hours.

"What's consensus war?" I asked.

"It means everyone wants it. Why do they have to draft guys to fight it, then? In Oakland there's going to be a war against the war. You'd better come to master class, where it's safe."

In a pouting voice I said, "You're going to tell my mother, aren't you?"

"Listen to me, Joanne! The police will crack some heads. Arrests will be made. Are you willing to go to jail?"

And cause my mom heart failure? I thought a moment. "But the protests help! The government is going to have to start paying attention to them." I looked up at him through the curtain of my parted hair, pleading with my eyes.

"Do what you have to do, then," he said in a resigned tone. "Just be careful. Stay in the back, and if things turn ugly, get out." He patted my shoulder before handing me my music. "Just one thing: How is this a *family* event?"

"Well, uh, remember me telling you about my brother?" I confided in Dr. Harold about everything.

"The one you don't like?"

"I've only got one—Dan. He's dying to get over to Nam to uh...die."

Dr. Harold rubbed his beard thoughtfully. "I see."

It was true I didn't want Dan killed, but I also didn't want him to have the chance to go off to war and be especially good at fighting it. I had overheard him talking to Pete about their friend Jimmy Howe and some other soldiers in his company who saved the ears of dead Vietcong as souvenirs. Dan bragged that once he got over to Nam, his ear collection would be the biggest. Going off to the Stop the Draft march, I was on a mission with a slogan: No ears for Dan!

It was easy for Martin and me to hitch a ride across the Bay Bridge. Streams of cars and buses were pouring into Berkeley from all directions. Fifteen thousand participants were expected, some coming from as far as Oregon.

Huddled in the back of a jammed VW van painted in

Day-Glo psychedelic designs, I asked Martin, "What if you get drafted? Will you go?"

"I'm not killing anybody. Not even the U.S. government can make me do that."

"You're willing to go to jail?"

"No."

"You're going to Canada or Mexico?"

He shook his head. "I'm dodging. If a law is unjust or immoral, it's my personal responsibility to break it. Civil disobedience— Henry David Thoreau wrote about it long before Gandhi and King put it into practice. There's enough guys who want to go to war without the draft."

I rolled my eyes. "Dan, for instance. Guys like him want to feel they're being brave, risking their lives to defend our country."

"They're brainwashed into believing that. The real reason is they're looking for adventure. They want to test their mettle, then boast about it later."

I laughed and said, "No ears for Dan!" Then I explained.

People streamed into Sproul Plaza on the campus of the University of California to assemble for the march. The majority were not hippies, as I had anticipated, but Cal students, the guys in trousers, oxford shirts, and corduroy jackets and the girls in jumpers, white blouses, and bobby socks. There were some older men in suits and ties, maybe professors. I thought with a chill across my nape that I could possibly run into Jerry and Denise. Good little Denise at a war protest? It didn't seem likely, but then Jerry was the boss of her now, and he was antiwar.

There were famous people there, including author Ken Kesey and Beat poet Allen Ginsberg. When a TV reporter asked Ginsberg what he thought of the gathering, he produced finger cymbals from his robe and accompanied himself in a chant. Country Joe and the Fish sang their "Feel Like I'm Fixin' to Die Rag" jug-band style, including washboard and kazoo, while the vast crowd clapped the beat and sang along on the chorus. Phil

Ochs was more pensive, accompanying his plaintive tenor on a single guitar, singing "I Ain't Marching Anymore."

One of the organizers came on the microphone to announce, "Today marks the first day of Stop the Draft Week. We are declaring a draft holiday for this time period. We are going to close the Oakland army induction building down. Today we are willing to be disruptive. Today is the movement from protest to resistance."

We all assembled in a broad column on Telegraph Avenue and began to march toward Oakland. Martin smiled at me and clasped my hand. "Here we go, Joni. Hold on tight."

A stranger took my other hand. All around us people were holding hands or linking arms. Some demonstrators carried pickets, STOP THE BOMBING, BRING THE BOYS HOME, NO MORE WAR, PEACE, GET U.S. OUT OF VIETNAM. A little boy riding his father's shoulder held an ARMS ARE FOR EMBRACING bumper sticker like a banner before his face. We sang "This little light of mine, I'm gonna let it shine." It made me feel like I mattered, that I, too, was a necessary part of this demonstration.

It was a good time until we reached the Oakland city line. Across the width of the street was a barrier of policemen dressed for combat, with helmets and billy clubs. Someone raised his palm and yelled, *"Heil!"* and we all joined in with a slow, driving rhythm.

*"Heil! Heil! Heil!"* I shouted to the fascist police, which refused to let us pass. I knew the Oakland policemen were merely doing what they were paid to do: keep peace and order in their city.

They forced us onto the sidewalk on one side of the street, thinned out to three abreast. On the other side of the street were the protesters protesting the protesters. "Traitors! Commies!" they yelled at us. "Why don't you go home?"

We pressed on, through a Negro slum, where black faces appeared in windows and doors and little kids sat in rows on their stoops to watch us pass. The line of buses filled with inductees rolled slowly through town, enveloped by a barricade of policemen, parading in a rectangular formation, their billy clubs at the ready. The faces of the inductees at the bus windows looked forlornly out at us. They were boys who had been called upon to serve their country, gazing out at their countrymen, who did not appreciate their sacrifice.

I wanted to break through the ranks of the cops, leap onto a bus, and start shoving those guys to the door, screaming, "Get out! Get out! They're sending you to your deaths!" Of course I couldn't. Of course I kept to the sidewalk.

A bus drew to a halt in front of the induction center, which had been covered with peace signs and three-foot-tall HELL NOS in bloodred poster paint. The police parted the demonstrators to make a clear pathway from the doors of the bus to the doors of the induction center. The demonstrators pumped their fists in unison, shouting, "Don't go! Don't go! Don't go!"

As the inductees filed by, dressed in trousers or jeans, all with short hair, some carrying overnight satchels, one of them grabbed the front of a protester's shirt and thrust his fist threateningly into the protester's face. Draftee and antidraft demonstrator were nose to nose, but the latter never flinched, still pleading, "Say no! You don't have to go!" The inductee gave him a final shove and moved on.

Bus after bus was unloaded right before our eyes, and not one of the inductees stepped out of line and joined our ranks. They believed they did have to go. They came from families who told them that if their country drafted them, they had to serve without questioning the reason or the morality. Not to serve meant shame, ingratitude for this country, and an unwillingness to protect freedom. Not to serve meant a guy was a yellow coward, a traitor—worst of all, a draft dodger, and such a label brought disgrace. Better to be a hero, dying in the rotting jungle of a country most of us had never heard of before the draft.

The buses had succeeded in safely delivering the draftees to the induction center, but they were going to have difficulty shipping them out. Beyond the building the protesters flooded the streets and faced the police battalion that had been guarding the buses. Too late I remembered Dr. Harold's warning to stay in back. The demonstrators surged. As I was pushed forward by a wall of bodies behind me, I felt Martin's hand slipping from mine. Only our clawing fingertips held on to each other, and then Martin was gone, shoved in one direction, and me in the other. In one frenzied mass the demonstrators pressed into the policemen, who lifted their batons. I wanted to shelter my skull in my hands, but I needed them to grope and clutch the shoulders of people in front of me. If I stumbled now, I would be trampled.

An amazing thing happened. As the demonstrators rushed forward, the policemen walked, then ran, backward, holding their billy clubs horizontally before them in defense. We were pushing farther and farther into downtown Oakland, the police falling back one block, two, three. We outnumbered them, and they were scared. We were winning the city.

If we couldn't stop the buses from coming in, we could stop them from leaving. Protesters dismantled the fences of the poor people who lived there to build barricades in the street. Others let air out of the tires of cars. A car that was rumored to belong to a federal district attorney was overturned. People rolled huge cement tubs holding small trees into the street. Where was Martin in all this? How would I find my way out of there without him?

A Negro woman standing by her car pleaded with the demonstrators who blocked it: "I've got to get to work." A kid about my age snatched at her keys. She slapped his face, and he recoiled. Another demonstrator tried to push people off her car. "Let the lady pass," he urged them. She got into her car and started it, but she was going nowhere, blocked by humanity.

The paddy wagons roared onto the scene from the other direction. When protesters were clubbed, they fell to the asphalt and curled into fetal positions, cradling their skulls in their arms. People who resisted arrest were dragged to the paddy wagons by their feet or were walked between two or three policemen, choked by billy clubs held across their throats. Cuffed protesters ran away, were caught, broke away, were caught again, each time with a more violent response by the police.

Antiprotesters broke into fistfights with protesters and held on to their clothes, helping the police arrest them. Finally, I spotted Martin, down on his back, being dragged by the ankles by two policemen. I rushed to his rescue, clutching him by the armpits. "Let go, miss," a policeman warned as he raised his billy club over my head. How much would it hurt? I wondered. Would it crack my skull? Would I ever be able to memorize Beethoven again?

My neck snapped back as I was yanked from behind by my hair, the billy club descending inches before me. I tried to twist around, fists swinging, as my captor held me fast.

"Stop struggling, Joanne!" Dan yelled at me. "I'm trying to save your life."

Trembling in fear and rage, tears and snot streaming down my face, I screamed back at him, "I'm trying to save yours!" I was so mad at him for being the stupid brother he was, I slugged him in the chest. He gave my hair another hard yank.

"Break it up, you two!" snarled a policeman, his hands digging into our shoulders.

"She's my sister!" Dan explained.

The policeman let his hands drop to his sides with a slap. "Okay, then."

Dan and Pete linked their arms in mine and escorted me to Pete's car, parked several blocks away. I went along sullenly but peacefully, relieved to be rescued. Every once in a while I looked back, hoping to catch sight of Martin. It seemed certain he'd been arrested and loaded into a paddy wagon.

When we got to Pete's car, a burgundy '64 Mustang, Pete flipped the front seat forward for me to climb into the back, and he and Dan settled in the front.

As Pete crept through traffic toward the Bay Bridge, Dan launched into his harangue. "Wait till I tell. Mommy's little girl committing treason and vandalism! You think those poor people can afford to replace their fences?"

"I never touched them."

"What do you think your little friends accomplished today? Huh? Buncha Commie pinko fags."

I stared out the window.

"Not a damn thing. Not a single one of those upstanding American boys fell out of line. Not a single one! It's kinda funny! All them hippie-type Commie pinko bed wetters running around doing nothing."

"They were Cal students, most of them."

"Students! Bullshit! Outside agitators the Communists sent over from China to overthrow the free world." Dan turned around in his seat and leered at me. "I saw him, Joanne. Your hippie boyfriend. The same guy I caught you with in the park."

"He's not my boyfriend."

"Are you fucking him?"

"No!" My face flushed with his nasty talk.

"Do you already have a love-child-type bun in the oven?"

"Shut up!"

"I'm telling Mom to take you to the doctor to check you out. Make sure your snatch isn't crawling with hippie-scum diseases."

I slid down and kicked him in the back through the seat of the car at the same time Pete jabbed an elbow into his ribs.

"Oof!" cried Dan, glaring at Pete. "What was that for?"

"You don't want to talk to your sister that way."

"You're telling me how I should talk to my sister?"

"No, I'm telling you what way you *don't* want to talk to her." Pete looked at me in the rearview mirror. "Easy on the car, Joanne. This is my baby." He patted the steering wheel for emphasis.

"Sorry, Pete." I wondered how my brother could have such a decent guy for a friend. "I'm telling our dad every word he said to me. I got major stuff on him to tell both my parents."

Dan tried to sneer at me over the top of his seat, but he looked guilty. "Like what?"

"When you start finking on me, it will all come out."

"You've got nothing on me." Traffic was picking up now, and we were almost to the tollbooth. Dan dug through the change in his pocket and handed Pete two quarters.

"Maybe you got Mom and Dad fooled, but I'm on to your game."

"My game? Oh, right." He laughed nervously, indicating I had him just where I wanted him. Another couple of beats of silence passed. Rolling his eyes back at me, he tried to sound nonchalant. "Like what?"

"I know you're flunking out of your classes on purpose so you'll get drafted, and then Mom and Dad will have to let you enlist in the marines."

He batted the air. "You're crazy."

We drove through the city in silence, and when we reached Haight and Masonic, Dan asked Pete to pull over. "We gotta drop Joanne here. It will look suspicious if we walk in the house together."

Pete veered toward the curb and stopped. Dan leaped out of the car and folded the seat forward. "Get out," he barked at me.

"So you can get a head start telling on me? No way!" I crossed my arms.

"Cripes, Joanne. You know I won't tell if you don't."

"Say you're sorry for all the dirty things you said to me. You know I don't do *it*."

Dan looked down at the sidewalk.

Pete ducked to look out at Dan. "Apologize."

"Dammit, Pete! Don't tell me what to do."

"Fine." Pete reached across the passenger seat, slammed the door, and laid an impressive patch as he pulled out. Out the back window, I saw Dan standing on the sidewalk, his mouth hanging open. I flashed him a peace sign; I couldn't resist. Pete drove me to the corner of Masonic and Frederick, leaving me less than a block to walk home.

"Thanks, Pete," I said, bailing out.

He looked sheepish, staring down at his hands and mumbling, "He shouldn't talk to you that way."

All afternoon I practiced scales and arpeggios, something mindless, something I could do with shaky fingers. Vivid scenes of the demonstration flashed in my head the march, the billy club over my head, Martin like a bug on his back about to be smashed. If only there were a way for me to know he was okay.

The phone rang for the second time in five minutes. My mother answered it. "You have the wrong number," she said. "Again!" She was making a pie, and when she set the receiver in place, her hand left a floury print on it. "Honestly! Looking for a guy named Phil Ochs."

The third time Martin called, I dove for the phone. "Hello?" I asked anxiously.

"I got away," he said breathlessly. "I gotta see you. I'm at the Tangerine Kangaroo."

"Okay. I'll be there. Bye!"

I darted through the kitchen, explaining, "It was Suyu. I forgot Daddy's pants again."

"Honestly, Joanne, if your head wasn't fastened on...Hold on, now. Get a few quarters out of my change purse."

I turned around and went to her purse on the kitchen counter.

"Funny how the Lis never gave a reminder call before."

"Oh, business is slow. Suyu wants to talk to me about master class."

"Well, don't take forever."

"I won't. Bye!"

I was out the back door in a flash and ran all the way to Haight and Ashbury. I rounded the corner and slammed into Martin's fierce hug. He was trembling.

"Thank God you're all right," he murmured into my ear. "I saw you leave with your brother."

I tried to push away, but he held on tighter, rocking us from side to side. Moments later, I tried again, but he still wouldn't let go.

"Martin! Let me see you."

"No."

I shoved away to look into his face. "God." His left eye was swollen shut, bruised purple and green. A red welt crossed his throat.

He grinned and winced. "You should see the other guy."

"I did. About three cops in combat gear. "

We went into the Tangerine Kangaroo and ordered tea at the counter. When we were settled at a table, Martin told me what had happened after I left. "They set me on my feet, and a cop got me into a choke hold with his billy club to escort me to a paddy wagon that was already packed. Then the cop guarding us got called away, so a bunch of us ran out. I just kept running until I was sure no one was chasing me."

I reached up and touched his hair next to his swollen eye. "Does it hurt?"

He nodded. "Not like they're hurting in Nam."

"We did it, didn't we? Stopped the war machine!" I spoke in a high-pitched, giddy voice that made Martin smile. "The government has got to listen to us now! Oakland looked like a war zone!"

"Except bombs weren't falling from the sky. Except children weren't running down the street with their backs on fire."

"But we made a difference, didn't we? The war is going to end sooner because of us!"

Martin stirred his tea thoughtfully. "Not soon enough. A lot more people are gonna die over there first."

I reached for his hand across the table. "My mom's going to wonder where I am. Sit and drink your tea. Maybe it will help you feel better."

He squeezed my hand. "You're what makes me feel better, Joni."

I didn't want to leave him, but I had to. I ran home and burst into the kitchen, the imprint of his battered face burning in my mind. Mom was taking her pie out of the oven, filling the kitchen with a delicious cinnamon-apple smell. She cocked her head and said, "Joanne," like a rebuke.

I slapped my forehead. The dry cleaning! I made an about-face and charged out of the house again.

\*　\*　\*

That night I couldn't sleep, with that cop's billy club descending, playing like a film loop in my mind. Had Dan really saved my life? Naw, the cops probably knew how to crack heads without killing people. I hated Dan for the filthy way he'd talked to me right in front of Pete. Like most girls my age, I thought of sex as the big mystery, something that would happen to me in the future. I wished that when it felt right for me to make love, it would be with Martin.

I sighed, rolled over, and squeezed my pillow tight against my body, pretending it was Martin. I loved Martin, and he loved me, but I knew I was the only one of us "in love." It was true what I said to Dan: Martin was not my boyfriend. He could not be possessed. I didn't know how he spent his time when he wasn't with me; I didn't want to know. Martin just had to be free. That was all anybody ever talked about. Even the Monkees had a song about it, "I Wanna Be Free." I didn't want to be free. I wanted to belong to Martin, and I wanted him to belong to me.

# CHAPTER
# THIRTEEN

My first scheduled performance at master class was drawing near. Musically, I was as ready as I could be; I had known my whole *"Pathétique"* sonata by heart for over three months. Physically, I was a wreck. On the outside, I appeared to be the same as usual, but somehow the core of my body knew I was performing. I had diarrhea. Occasionally I broke out in shivers.

What, really, was a memorized piece? I couldn't see it or touch it or explain it. It consisted of scales and chords and rote motor motions. Whenever I was on the verge of forgetting, I felt it first in my fingers: some minute motion was not the same as I had practiced, a slip off a key or a miscalculated sweep of the arm. Sometimes a sound such as rattling silverware in the kitchen blocked the information that flowed from brain to fingers. It was a dicey operation, when I was hoping for perfection.

Mom was in a dither about her upcoming Thanksgiving dinner, and already she was churning the wheels of the massive assembly line that would crank out over two hundred Christmas cards. Arriving home from school, I would find her at her desk in the den, amid several TV trays piled with stationery, photographs, stamps, and Christmas seals. Relatives and closest family friends merited a handwritten letter and photographs of us kids, other friends rated just the letter, and the neighbors and Dad's business associates got "Merry Christmas and Happy New Year from Dick, Helen, Dan, and Joanne," written with a flourish in my mother's finest penmanship. It was sad that Denise, a married woman now, was excluded this year, as if there had been a death in the family.

The day of the class arrived, and I discovered I was last on the program. While the other three students performed, the seat I had saved next to me for Martin remained empty. When it was finally my turn, I feared my legs would collapse under me on my walk to the front of the room. Seated at the piano, I raised my hands to play and felt that the bench was too high. I was too nervous to crank it down, but Dr. Harold stopped me to adjust the bench himself. Little titters of laughter rose in the room, which set me at ease. All my peers in the studio were with me, hoping I would play well. The door opened and closed and light footsteps tapped across the hardwood floor. Without looking up, I knew that Martin was with me, too.

I sank the weight of my arms into the first, tragic C minor chord. The action of the piano was stiff, which would make it harder to articulate fast runs, and the vast room, with its vaulted ceiling and those hardwood floors, caused the sound to bounce around and confuse my ears. I made it through the first page, then flubbed the first run. That's okay, I thought. Now I no longer needed to worry about making the first mistake. But I continued to make mistakes, so that the development section was an absolute tangle. The worst is over, I thought at the end of the first movement. I settled comfortably into the slow, melodious second movement, and even the triplet section with the bumpy thumb accompaniment turned out smooth. Then, in the third movement, I forgot. My hands frantically roved over the keyboard, not knowing where I was in the music or how to pick it up again. I started the section over, and with shaking fingers managed to complete my performance. It was over, and I had made a mess of it.

The audience applauded politely, except for one person, who cupped his palms to clap the loudest and the longest, a sweet gesture by Martin that increased my embarrassment. Dr. Harold began to discuss my performance and asked me to try various techniques in several sections. I responded woodenly, with a frightened grin stretched across my face. Finally, mercifully, the session was over. I rose from the piano, walked down the aisle, snatched my music satchel from my seat, and, looking straight ahead, scurried out the door and plunged down Nob Hill.

I heard running footsteps behind me. "Joni! Joni! Wait up!" Martin rushed to my side and put his arm around me, slowing me down by cupping my shoulder in his hand. "Wow! You really blew my mind!"

Of course he would say that. He had an untrained ear, and he wished the best for me. "I forgot," I said in a flat, angry tone. "Three whole seconds passed and I didn't play a note. I had to start the section over, and did you hear how I missed some of the runs? Oh, Martin, I forgot!" Finally the tears I had been holding back burst forth.

He held me, his forehead pressed against mine. "Don't be so hard on yourself, Joni. You had soul! There were sparks of genius!"

I pulled my head away from his. "Just sparks?"

"Well, yeah. Here and there. When you were able to forget you were in the spotlight and the audience melted away, and it was just you in the music. Do that all the time, and you'll be great."

"Yeah?" I said hopefully. Trained or untrained, Martin was a natural musician, and I was not.

"You care too much what people think of you. Forget 'em. Do your own thing."

"But how?"

"You've got to live in the moment. You've got to live like everything matters and nothing matters, all at the same time."

I knew this was some of his I Ching mumbo jumbo. "That makes no sense."

"You can care a lot, but when things don't work out like you hoped, just accept it, and try again the next time." He framed my face in his hands and wiped my tears away with his thumbs.

He smiled at me sadly, then kissed me. "I'm glad I finally got to hear you play. It was beautiful. You're beautiful, Joni."

When I got home, my mother hailed me from the den. "How did it go, Joanne?"

I ignored her. I sat at the piano and played my Beethoven straight through nearly flawlessly. Why I couldn't do that at master class, I didn't know.

At my next lesson, Dr. Harold didn't say anything about my performance, and I didn't mention it. I handed him my Beethoven, and he said, "Let's start with the Chopin nocturne today."

After that, he spent nearly a half hour helping me voice my Bach fugue. Time was running out. As he was wrapping up on Bach, I reached for my sonata again.

"I want you to give Beethoven a rest," he said.

"I can't! I'm going to play it next month on the Palace of Fine Arts program."

"Joanne, I'm taking you off that program."

I dropped my head and felt a tear trickle down my nose. It was humiliating to cry in front of my teacher, but the disappointment was too great.

"I'm sorry. I had reservations when I saw you sign up for the program. I should have said something then. Then at master class—"

"I was horrible, wasn't I?"

"Not at all. You had some dazzling moments."

It was exactly what Martin had said, but it was no consolation. I felt my shoulders shaking with my sobs. I wouldn't be performing at the Palace of Fine Arts after all, and I was too devastated to move. Dr. Harold handed me a Kleenex.

"I bet you're sorry you have me as a student."

"I'm honored to have you for a student, Joanne," he said quietly. "Put the musicians on the top of the ladder and the technicians on the bottom, and you'll find yourself several rungs higher. It would be wrong of me to allow you to perform in public before you're ready."

"I could get ready if you'd let me," I said hopefully. "I could practice more, hours and hours."

"You're giving Beethoven a rest," he said firmly. "I've got something for you." From his filing cabinet he removed a thin, yellow Schirmer publication. "I'm assigning you a new piece."

I read the front cover: RAVEL SONATINE. It sounded like "saltine." "Who's *Rav*el?"

"It's Ra*vel*."

"Who's that?"

"You're about to find out. Beethoven's *"Pathétique"* is a very popular piece, you know. Several of my students are working on it, but this piece is just for you. I'm going to ask you not to listen to any recordings. I want you to make this piece your own."

I opened it up to a swirl of complicated sixty-fourth notes. The third movement was ten pages long and marked *"Animé."* I knew enough French to know that meant fast. The Ravel looked hard, hard, hard. Another thing to fail at.

I wiped my eyes and stood. Dr. Harold must have had a schedule change, because waiting at the door was Suyu. I watched the way he smiled at her. It was not how he looked at me. She was special to him, his star, while I was just a blubbering goof-up.

When I got home, I threw the Ravel on top of the piano with the mess of music there. Then I went into the den, where my mother was, and burst into tears again as I told her what had happened at my lesson.

"I don't understand your Dr. Harold at all. First he tells you you can play at the Palace of Fine Arts, and then he goes back on his word. He's not being the least bit fair to you."

I didn't correct her by saying I had signed up to play without his saying anything about it.

"Heavens, Joanne! I never should have agreed to your taking lessons from him." She waved her hand at the stack of cards, addressed and stamped, waiting to be mailed. "Do you realize how many people I've told about your performance? I've already mailed a hundred cards!"

*　*　*

I didn't sleep well; I had nightmares about performing. In one dream the keys on the piano were rearranged so that I couldn't find the ones I needed. In another, the audience held a program of pieces I had forgotten to practice. The night before Thanksgiving, I woke up and began to play Beethoven's *"Pathétique"* sonata in my mind. I got out of bed, put on my bathrobe, and crept downstairs. I sat at the piano, lit by the streetlight, and went through the motions of playing over the tops of the keys. A few times I accidentally sounded a note, but very softly.

I started, having spotted out of my peripheral vision a ghostly figure perched on the edge of the sofa. It was my mother, in her nightgown, her face glistening with cold cream and her hairnet stuffed with Kleenex to prevent her weekly beauty-parlor bubble from flattening out in her sleep.

"Joanne," she said forlornly, "it's the middle of the night."

"Sorry. I was just checking this one part."

"Allowing you to take piano lessons from Dr. Harold was a mistake. It's too much for you. You're too high-strung. I can't bear to see my own daughter so unhappy."

"But, Mom, these have been the happiest three months of my life!"

"If you think this is happiness, you're headed for a miserable life! I worry you'll never be able to settle down like your sensible sister and be content with everyday life."

I swiveled to face her. "Mom! I am content! I love my life and the piano and Dr. Harold, and if you take that away from me I'll die!"

Mom sighed. "I'm not suggesting you quit piano. I only think that if you go back to Mrs. Scudder—"

A clatter from the back porch caused the house to shake like an earthquake had struck.

"The turkey!" Mom exclaimed in horror. Snoopy must have knocked down our Thanksgiving turkey, wrapped in tea towels and thawing on the washing machine.

We both ran through the kitchen onto the back porch to find a drunken Dan, sprawled on the linoleum amid a half dozen broken flowerpots, plants, and dirt. Dan struggled to find his feet and fell back on his butt before hurling chunks down the front of his jacket.

I looked at Mom. "And you're worried about me?"

Thanksgiving was a dreary day, pouring rain. Mom complained that I had missed some spots of tarnish when I had polished the silverware and had slathered too much pimento cheese spread on the celery sticks. I wasn't quite certain what she meant when she called me high-strung, but I was pretty sure I'd inherited the trait from her. As soon as Jerry and Denise arrived, Mom banished me from the kitchen, exclaiming that I was "underfoot," but I knew it was only so she could rant to Denise about my recent failure as a pianist.

I wandered into the den, where Dad, Dan, and Jerry were watching the Forty-Niners, leaning forward on their seats, clutching the necks of their beer bottles, and hooting and hollering. I didn't understand why it was so crucial that grown men knocked each other down in various formations and I didn't care, but Martin had once speculated that without football there would be a lot more war.

I sauntered over to Mom's desk and read one of the Christmas cards she had lying open.

Dear Ralston and Valentine,

How's the weather in Michigan? Denise is now happily married to one Jerry Westfield, a soon-to-be psychotherapist. This is hush-hush, but from the looks of it, we're soon to have a bouncing baby grandchild! Our Dan is attending San Francisco City College as a business major, following in the footsteps of his daddy. Our Joanne will be performing at the Palace of Fine Arts this December. As Dick says, "We count our blessings."

Merry Christmas and Happy New Year,

Dick, Helen, Dan, and Joanne

P.S. Dick complains about our dance lessons after working on his feet all day, but he just signed us up for another eight. Go figure!


Who were these people, Ralston and Valentine? Would my parents ever see them again? All around the world people were telling lies in their Christmas cards to people they hardly remembered. In my mother's case, they weren't exactly lies; she just didn't know what her family was really about. Was that true of most mothers? I had an urge to revise the whole thing:

Dear Ralston and Valentine,

Why would I be writing to some people in Michigan that we never see? Denise is now unhappily married to one Jerry Wienerfield, who won't let her go to college and complains she has immature clitoral orgasms. This is hush-hush, but our Dan is a drunk, flunking out of San Francisco City College, and from the looks of it will soon be a casualty in Vietnam. Our Joanne is the biggest failure of them all, having forgotten her Beethoven, so she won't be performing at the Palace of Fine Arts. As Dick says, "No one in this family has any talent."

P.S. Dick is just another word for penis. Go figure!


I wandered into the living room and flung myself on the sofa, looking over its back out the bay window. Martin was planning to hitchhike to spend the day with his Santa Cruz friends. I wondered if he'd gotten a ride or if he was standing on Highway 1 in the pouring rain. Why didn't he want to spend Thanksgiving with Gus, his only relative in California?

I felt a presence in the room and turned to find Denise standing before the piano. I could see why Mom thought she was pregnant; she'd gained weight, and although she'd never had acne as a teenager, her face was splotchy with zits. She wore a shapeless long skirt and a V-necked, grandfatherly brown cardigan, the front pockets sagging. Her hair was done up in a librarian's bun, and it was greasy.

"Did you ever think you couldn't do it, Joanne?" she asked. "I mean, you get so nervous at recitals. Why do you like to play the piano so much, anyway? Maybe you could try something else."

I looked at her for a long moment. "Like what? Typing letters?"

"Oh! That is so mean!" She plunged her fists into her sweater pockets and stalked back to the kitchen.

I looked out the window some more. I felt the weight of someone sinking into the sofa beside me. It was Jerry. He had greasy hair, too. Couldn't they afford shampoo? "Hi, Beethoven," he said, forcing a cheerful tone.

"Don't call me that," I snapped.

A long moment of silence passed. "I think you should stick with it," he said quietly. "It's part of you."

I kept staring out the window like I wasn't paying attention to him. Maxine Fulmer was coming up the walkway with Quentin Allen, whom Mom referred to as "Maxine's star boarder." Mom didn't seem to have much in common with Maxine anymore, but then Maxine and Quentin probably had no other place to go. Her kids were far away, a married son who practiced law somewhere on the East Coast and a daughter in the Peace Corps in Kenya.

My parents greeted their guests in the foyer, and Maxine handed Mom a plastic-wrapped tofu loaf shaped like a miniature roasted turkey, which I doubted anyone would touch, even Maxine.

Quentin was wearing a beautiful maroon Edwardian suit with a flowered vest, a pink-and-white-striped dress shirt, and a purple-and-pink paisley wide tie. It made me think how boring men's clothes usually were. He stood behind Maxine and attempted to slide off her raincoat.

"I'm not helpless," she scolded. More and more, "liberated" women were biting the heads off men who dared to open doors or pull out chairs for them, gestures that had traditionally been considered gentlemanly displays of respect for the weaker sex.

Quentin was not the least bit ruffled. "Of course you aren't helpless, my dear, but one ensconced in a coat is not as well positioned for said coat removal as another caring individual standing by to lend a hand. It is an honor and privilege for me to offer this simple act of kindness to one who has given me so much."

She patted his cheek. "You are a dear, Quentin."

My dad cleared his throat as if he were an embarrassed observer of a lovers' quarrel. "Well! What wet weather we're having!"

At dinner, Maxine talked about the 1968 presidential election, which was a whole year away. My parents weren't political. They were Democrats who voted in every election, and Dad was a big union man, but other than that they were pretty conservative. They complained that taxes were too high and believed that all people on welfare were too lazy to work. They weren't so much for the Vietnam War as they were disgusted by those who protested it.

"If only Bobby Kennedy would run," Maxine said. "He'd stop the war. I'll bet he throws his name in the ring yet."

"That would make no sense," said Jerry. "Eugene McCarthy is our antiwar candidate."

Maxine went on and on about Bobby as if she hadn't heard Jerry. As attorney general, Bobby had done so much for civil rights, and Bobby had taken on organized crime, and Bobby would fight for the redwoods and end poverty, and Bobby this and Bobby that.

"It's a moot point, Max," said Dad. "The incumbent is always nominated at the Democratic convention, and the incumbent is Johnson."

"And LBJ is doing a hell of a job!" exclaimed Dan.

"Yeah, bombing the hell out of Hanoi," said Jerry.

"Of course!" said Dan. "That's how we'll win. We can't withdraw from Vietnam without winning. It would be a waste!"

What he really meant was that the U.S. couldn't leave before he had a chance to get mixed up in the war. No ears for Dan, I still hoped. I didn't say much. I stuffed myself with turkey, cranberry sauce, dressing, mashed potatoes, marshmallow-topped sweet potatoes, and two kinds of pie: pumpkin and black bottom.

After the dishes were cleared and the dishwasher was humming, Maxine asked me to play something for her.

"I don't really feel like it," I said.

"Go on," said Mom, carting the heavy, grease-filled roaster from the stove to the sink. "Denise and I will finish up. Play your Beethoven for Maxine, Joanne."

I hadn't touched my Beethoven since the day of that fateful master class, but once I was seated at the piano, I played my heart out, just for Maxine. In my peripheral vision I could see her gently swaying, her eyes half-closed, her lids fluttering.

I had not released the final dying chord before everyone but Mom entered the room without giving Maxine time to compliment my playing. She didn't need to. That she had listened was enough. Maxine looked at Denise and patted the empty place next to her on the sofa. When Denise took the seat, Maxine launched into a tirade about how her "brothers," meaning men, had stood by her during the civil rights movement and the antiwar movement, but now for the women's movement, they had fled. From across the room, Jerry glared at Maxine's hairy legs flashing beneath her long brocade skirt.

I was so restless, I had to get out of the overheated room. I ran out the back door, flinging on my car coat, and dashed down Frederick Street in the cool drizzle. Just because I couldn't explain to Denise why I loved the piano, that didn't invalidate my feelings for it. I hurt inside so badly that not even Martin could console me. In fact, he made me mad. He had all the talent in the world, and he didn't even bother to learn to read music.

Maybe I was a little jealous of him, too. Would I ever learn to relax into the music the way he did, or would every performance of mine be sheer agony and misery?

Of all people, I appreciated Jerry the most. He was right; the piano was part of me. Who would I be if I quit? Who would be walking down the street or into a classroom? Just a shell of me, lacking purpose and passion and a goal. Without the piano, I would simply not be me.

With that resolved, I turned around and dashed back home.

# CHAPTER
# FOURTEEN

It happened on a day when I had a dentist appointment and had to make up a history quiz at lunch. Rena sat with Lisa Girardi and the in-crowd kids. The next day when I got to lunch, she was already at their table. I walked right by them as if they didn't exist, or at least I tried to.

"Hey, Donnelly, where'd you get that neat Nehru jacket?" Candy shouted after me. "It looks just like George Harrison's."

I stopped. "It doesn't look anything like his. My mother made it for me, and it's one of a kind."

"I'm sure glad my mother doesn't dress me," said Candy.

"Here's a spot for you right here, Joanne," Rena said hopefully, patting the bench next to her. I walked on as if I didn't hear her.

It was a long lunch period. I scarfed my food in about five minutes, and to keep from feeling self-conscious about sitting alone, I did my chemistry homework. After school, I didn't wait for Rena and started home alone. There's a saying that the women of San Francisco have the most shapely legs in the world, and as I angrily puffed up the big hill on Haight, my calves were burning!

I heard Rena behind me, shouting, "Joanne! Wait!" When she caught up, she said breathlessly, "Don't be mad."

"You can sit with whoever you want at lunch."

"But you're mad, even though I saved a spot for you. Lisa

isn't even going steady with Kent anymore. She has a new boyfriend from St. Ignatius."

"I don't care who Lisa dates."

"She's changed! She wears bell-bottoms and love beads."

"I don't care what she wears."

"I don't get you, Joanne. Sitting alone is social suicide. I can't stand it."

"I don't like the in-crowd kids. I'm not going to let them hurt my feelings anymore. What's so bad about that?"

"You've changed, Jo. Ever since you started hanging around with that hippie."

"His name is Martin, and this has nothing to do with him." It did, though. The way Martin built me up gave me the power to shun the in crowd. "You've changed, too, Rena."

"How?" she asked defensively.

I lifted a shoulder and let it drop. It would be too painful to go into it. For one thing, I didn't seem to matter to her anymore. All she talked about was herself and the theater. It had built her up in different way, giving her the power to claim a place in the in crowd.

When I didn't answer, Rena said, "Lisa's not so bad."

Maybe she wasn't. I let that drop, too.

Our friendship survived, but it wasn't the same, I felt, and Rena must've felt it, too. Sometimes I had lunch with the orchestra kids, but more often I ate alone. I realized if I did my homework during lunch, I'd have more time to practice at home.

One day I looked up from my history book to see Lisa standing before me. "I heard you know Gus Abbott. His brother is your boyfriend."

"I don't have a boyfriend."

"Rena says you go there, to the house where Roach lives. Could you take me to meet them sometime?"

I screwed up my mouth as if I was considering this. "Um, no."

"You probably don't even know them."

"Probably not."

Lisa stalled, thinking of another tack, while my heart beat fast. She was used to getting what she wanted, and it took effort to resist her. She gazed across the quad and noticed Suyu sweeping her arms apart, lost in the music in her head. "Oh, my God, what is that Oriental freak doing?"

"That's Suyu Li. She's a great pianist."

"Well, there isn't a piano there." Lisa cupped her mouth and shouted, "Hey, Chop Suyu, stop that weird thing you're doing. You're embarrassing the whole school!"

Suyu looked over at us and put her hands in her lap. Now it was up to me to set things right. I started walking the gauntlet of all the other tables. The nerds, the jocks, the band kids, the Negroes, Mexicans, Puerto Ricans, Japanese, and Koreans all stared at me as I passed them, and then I was standing before Suyu.

"Hi, Joanne."

"Hi, Suyu. I'm sorry about what Lisa just yelled."

"It's okay. Your friend doesn't matter to me."

"She's not my friend. She just uses me."

"What does that mean, use you?"

"You know, she only comes around when she wants something."

"Friends help each other, right?"

"Well, yeah." I felt heat surge up my neck, making my jacket feel too hot. It occurred to me that I only sought out Suyu when I needed help with my piano. At school we traveled in different circles. She took calculus and physics rather than orchestra and choir, and if I ever joined her and her Chinese friends, it would just seem too weird. "Well, anyways, I just want to say sorry for how rude Lisa was."

Suyu shrugged. "It's nothing. She is nothing."

Right then Suyu taught me something that had nothing to do with piano. Lisa had power over me only because I gave it to her.

When Christmas vacation came, I was relieved to forget about school cliques. I got to practice the piano more and to see more of Martin, my two favorite things. I also babysat.

I never minded babysitting; I liked it. Sitting on the couch with two or three kids watching the same TV programs I did at home, *Batman, I Dream of Jeannie, Hogan's Heroes, Gilligan's Island*, playing an occasional hand of crazy eights or helping to button a dress on a doll—what was hard about that? It was good money, fifty cents an hour. After the kids went to bed I could have whatever food I wanted. There was usually a record collection or some sexy books tucked away in a bookcase, and sometimes there was even a piano.

New Year's Eve 1967, I was hired by the Johnsons up on East Yerba Buena. Martin was out of town, traveling as a roadie with Roach, who had a big gig in L.A. that night. After I put the kids to bed, I turned off the TV and turned on KYA to listen to the countdown of the top hundred hits of '67, timed so that number one would be aired at midnight. I was excited about finding out how high on the chart Roach's "Evolution! Revolution!" would rank. Every time a song came on that wasn't Roach, I cheered, knowing they would be that much higher on the list.

It was a little before ten o'clock, only at hit number twenty-six, and I had just settled in the easy chair with a handful of Oreos, when I heard Mr. and Mrs. Johnson coming through the back door. I dumped the cookies in my bag, dusted off my lap, and stood to greet them. Mr. Johnson wasn't feeling well, the old fuddy-duddy, and instead of a whopping four dollars, Mrs. Johnson handed me only two. Two bucks on New Year's Eve! Didn't they realize I had turned down three other jobs to sit for them?

To make matters worse, when Mrs. Johnson drove me home, I found our house lit up and half a dozen cars in our narrow drive, reminding me that my parents were at a dinner dance at a hotel on Union Square, which included a champagne breakfast, and they wouldn't be returning until morning. They had given Dan permission to "have a few friends over" to celebrate Jimmy Howe's being home on leave from Vietnam. I just hoped Jimmy hadn't brought along his ear collection to gross me out and stink up our house.

Jimmy was a scrawny guy with red hair and freckles. I

wouldn't say he was poor, but he lived with only his mom down on Page Street, where the Victorians were run-down and the front doors opened out onto the sidewalk. His mom supported them by working as a checker at Safeway, when most moms didn't have jobs. He'd been a year ahead of Dan and Pete in school, so they looked up to him. Jimmy wasn't much of a student, and right out of high school his mom had gotten him a job stocking shelves at Safeway. A few months after that, he got drafted.

"Looks like your parents are throwing a big party," said Mrs. Johnson.

"My brother. Night, Mrs. Johnson."

"Happy New Year, Joanne," she replied as I got out of the car.

From the street I could hear Big Brother and the Holding Company on the stereo, Janis Joplin screeching out, "Piece of My Heart." My plan was to walk straight through the house and up the stairs to my room, so I could lie on my bed, eat my Oreos, and continue listening to the countdown.

In the kitchen, six girls were crowded around the table, probably to avoid the war talk going on in the living room. They were dipping into a platter of Rice Krispies Treats and washing them down with shots of tequila. I wondered who was going to clean up the vomit.

The living room was thick with smoke, which my mom would complain about later. She and Dad had quit years ago, when Dad started hacking for about an hour every morning when he got up. They must have known that Dan and a lot of his friends smoked. About four couples were dancing, while a group of guys were arguing loudly about who was going to the Super Bowl. Dan was sprawled on the sofa, passed out, his mouth gaping open. I knew he had started drinking at noon.

I kicked his shoe and said, "The life of the party."

Sitting next him, Pete said, "He's just resting. He'll come to in a while." From the can he was holding, Pete poured a trickle of beer on Dan's forehead, and Dan swatted at it, causing uproarious laughter. A girl who was perched on the arm of the sofa slid into Pete's lap and started making out with him. End of conversation.

I went upstairs and pushed open my door. Amid the coats and purses that had been piled on Denise's bed, someone stirred. I thought for an embarrassing instant that I had walked in on a couple making love. But by the bathroom night-light across the hall, I could see that it was just one body, a guy, with Snoopy curled in a ball over his feet.

He rolled over and looked at me. "Oh, hi, Joanne."

"Hi, Jimmy." The guest of honor. I almost didn't recognize him. He looked a lot older and even thinner, probably because of all that marching around in rice paddies he did and because C rations didn't taste that good.

"I guess this is your room, isn't it? I came upstairs to take a leak, and this little bed looked so damn inviting."

"Like Goldilocks?"

"Huh? Oh. Yes, ma'am. I'm just so damn tired. Do you mind if I rest here a few more minutes?"

"I guess not." I did mind, actually. I switched on the small lamp on my nightstand. "I want to listen to the KYA top hundred countdown."

"The what, ma'am? Oh, far out, let's you and me listen to the countdown."

I kicked off my shoes, pushed some coats out of my way, and sat on my bed, propped against the pillows. I turned on my radio and out came "Incense and Peppermints" by the Strawberry Alarm Clock.

"This is a groovy song." Jimmy rolled onto his back, closed his eyes, and clasped his hands across his middle—the pose of a dead man in his coffin. It gave me the willies.

"Can you hear American rock in Vietnam?"

"Yes, ma'am."

"Don't ma'am me, Jimmy. You make me feel like an old lady."

"Sorry, it's my training."

126

The DJ announced, "Number twenty-two, 'White Rabbit.'"
I got excited that Roach had beat the Airplane.

Jimmy swung his feet to the floor and patted his jacket pocket. "Mind if I smoke?"

"Naw."

I was surprised when he withdrew a joint. He lit it and inhaled. He shook out the match, then looked for a place to put it. I handed him a sand candle, the best I could do for an ashtray. "Do you get high?" he asked.

"Sometimes." He offered me the joint and I took a hit. "So how come you're not downstairs with Dan and those guys showing off your ears?" His eyes got wide and I laughed, partly because of the high. "You know, all those ears you whacked off the VC. Dan says you have a whole collection."

"Shit." He shook his head. "I had one. Won it in a poker game and traded it for a kilo. Gettin' high is the only way this war is bearable."

I giggled. "Isn't that kinda dangerous? Like, can you shoot straight if you get into a fight?"

"There are no fights. The truth is, ma'am, we never see old Charlie. Sniper bullets whiz by our heads, yeah. Bouncing Betty springs up on the trail, yeah. No Charlie in sight."

I couldn't stop laughing. "Betty sounds like a fun girl."

"No, ma'am, not fun. It's a mine equipped with a spring, so that it bounces up to midchest before detonating. When guys are blown away like that their buddies go around looking in the bushes for chunks of them to load into the body bag."

The laugh I was on got lodged in my throat. Was that the origin of "blown away"? One moment a GI was whole, and the next he was gone? "If you don't fight, what do you do?"

"Go on patrol. Search the villages for VC. There are just poor rice farmers, you know, but the villages are nearly empty. Sometimes just a few cows and chickens. Sometimes a few women, children, and old men. We pull the old men out of their huts and beat them up, trying to get them to tell us where the VC are hiding, but they never tell us nothing. You look into them sloped eyes, and you can just see they hate us. They don't seem to get we're saving them from the Commies. Then we burn down the village so the VC can't use it."

"Where are the VC?"

"Hiding in tunnels. Hell, they were dug in long before we got there. And it's going to get worse before it gets better. The war is spreading to other countries."

"It is?"

"Look." He set my Beethoven and Bach statuettes side by side. He pointed to Beethoven and said, "This is North Vietnam, where the Commies are." He tapped Bach. "This is South Vietnam, where we're trying to keep the Commies from taking over." He reached over and set Schumann and Chopin next to the other two composers. "Here are the countries Laos and Cambodia, Vietnam's neighbors to the west. Since South Vietnam is so heavily armed, the VC are cutting through these two countries on the Ho Chi Minh Trail to get to the south. We're starting to bomb there, too."

"How will we win?"

Jimmy shook his head. "Unless we change the way we're fighting this thing, I don't think we will."

I fluttered my fingers toward the stairs. "That isn't what you tell Dan and Pete and those other guys."

"Oh, well. I tell the college boys what they want to hear. I'm their war hero only because they want me to be. Hopefully this mess will be over by the time they're graduated and they'll never have to serve."

"Dan wants to go, real bad."

"I know. I hope he doesn't. Tell him to stay in school, Joni. Keep him safe at home."

"I go by Joanne."

"Joanne," he said.

We fell silent, listening to the radio. Number twenty-one was "Evolution! Revolution!" Not bad, but I wished it were higher. Next came "Never My Love," by the Association, the kind of song you listen to in the darkness with the one you love. I thought of Martin. Jimmy I didn't think had anyone.

When the song was over, he stretched and stood. "It's been good talking to you, Joanne. I've only known you as Dan's kid sister, but you're a real nice girl."

"Thanks."

"I have a favor to ask. Would you write me?"

"I . . . guess. What about?"

"Oh, nothing special. What you watched on TV, what your mom cooked for dinner, what's in bloom in the park. I'd be glad to hear anything about home."

"Sure, that's easy." He wrote down his address, and we hugged good-bye. "Take care of yourself, Jimmy."

"I'll do my best." Then he was gone, shuffling down the stairs in the darkness.

# CHAPTER FIFTEEN

I held two tickets under Lisa Girardi's pert, twice-whacked nose. On them was printed FILLMORE AUDITORIUM, FEBRUARY 21, THE PURPLE COCKROACH AND THE GRATEFUL DEAD. Lisa reached for them, and I whisked them behind my back. Her eyes bugged.

"Are you taking Rena?" Her breath was milky in the cold air as we stood in front of the school just before the first bell.

"She's got a rehearsal." Besides performing in *The Crucible*, Rena was in rehearsal with another company as the second-to-oldest sister in *The Sound of Music*. I didn't know she could sing, but her mother had hired a voice coach. I hardly ever saw Rena out of school now. "Here's the plan," I told Lisa. "We'll say we're going to the school dance together that night."

"Not the Fillmore?"

"We've got to tell our parents something. I have to leave home at six, so that means I'll have to tell my mom I'm eating at your house."

Lisa's eyes darted around. "I'll have to ask my mom."

"No, dammit. That's what I'm going to *tell* my mom. Don't worry. I won't be setting foot in your house."

"You don't have to put it like that." Lisa looked a lot different now, skinny and twitchy. She'd stopped bleaching her hair, and with her wide, dark eyes peering out from behind masses of black hair, she looked like a confused child. Her new boyfriend had lots of money for drugs. Both he and Lisa were speed freaks. When I handed her the tickets, she asked, "*Both* of them? I thought we were going together."

"Nope. I'm going to sneak in with the band."

"You mean Roach? You'll introduce me?"

"I didn't say that."

She eased her suede-fringed bag off her shoulder. "How much do I owe you?"

"They're comps. Martin gave them to me."

"Well, how much do you want me to pay you for them?"

"Nothing. Just stick with our story, okay?"

Lisa's forehead creased. It was hard to stay focused when you were on bennies.

"I'm coming to your house for dinner, and we're going to the school dance together. If anybody asks, that's what you tell them."

"Got it." She gave me a weak smile. "Joanne? I want to give you something in return."

"You don't have to."

"I want to." She dug around in her purse for a few minutes and then laid in my palm a square of cardboard, smaller than a postage stamp. "Here."

It was a blotter, which had absorbed a drop of liquid containing LSD. Not knowing the manufacturer or how potent the dose, I didn't want it, but how uncool would it be to reject acid from the most popular girl in school? My fingers closed around it, and I dropped it into my book satchel. "Thanks."

When I turned to leave, Lisa called after me, "I really do like you, Joanne. I know you don't think so, but I do."

The night of the dance, I went over to Martin's, where I changed into my jeans and one of his work shirts and tucked my hair under a baseball cap. We rode over to the Fillmore in the van with Roach and all their equipment. Gus was in a foul mood because they were opening for the Dead.

"Just once I'd like it to be the other way around," he muttered.

I was glad about the arrangement because the Fillmore dances lasted until two and I had to leave at eleven, when high school dances ended, and of course I'd rather see the Purple Cockroach perform than the Grateful Dead.

My roadie disguise worked fine. No one questioned who I was as I carried microphones, cords, and other equipment from the van to the stage. While Martin helped stack the tower of amplifiers and test for sound, I wandered around checking things out.

The Fillmore was a huge ballroom with a balcony running its length. The light-show dudes were setting up screens, projectors, black lights, strobe lights, and thunder machines. When the doors opened, Roach began the first set. The room filled with hot, flailing bodies, and I got thirsty. I went looking for Martin backstage and found a thermos belonging to the band. I opened it and sniffed it, expecting it to be whiskey, but to my delight it was cold, sweet orange juice. I poured myself a cup and screwed the top back on.

I found Martin standing in front of the stage, where the music was deafening.

I nudged his shoulder and shouted, "It's hot in here, and I couldn't find a drinking fountain."

"There's some juice in the cooler backstage. Just don't drink out of Bread's thermos."

I stared back at him, rubbing the corner of my mouth. "Uh...how come?"

He pointed his chin toward the stage door, through which I had just exited. "You drank from it, didn't you? Damn, you shouldn't go around downing other people's stuff without knowing what's in it."

"What is in it?" I screamed over the music, at the moment it stopped. But I already knew Bread's reputation as an acid freak. "Oh, God." I pressed my hand over my mouth.

"Well, Joni, you've been wanting to try acid. Have a good trip." He gave me a little smirk and a shake of his head. "You can't go home tonight."

I put my arms around him and spoke in his ear. "I'm afraid."

"Just go with the flow. I'm here for you, Joni. I won't let anything bad happen to you."

How could he promise me that? The journey I was about to take was through my own mind. How could Martin control my thoughts? I held him tight. I felt our clothes fuse together. We were wearing the same pants, the same shirt, the same skin. "Will you drop acid, too?" I asked.

"No. I'll be your guide. It's the safest way. Now let's go find a pay phone."

Martin took my hand, and as he led me across the dance floor, we bumped into Lisa and her new boyfriend.

"Joanne! Isn't this far out? Thanks for the tickets! Did you try that blotter I gave you?"

"Uh, not yet."

"I've had two!" Lisa's pupils were like saucers.

I stared straight into her face. "You don't have a nose. There's just an empty cavity where your nose should be. Just like a skull."

Lisa clapped both hands over the center of her face and screamed. Someone laughed. It was a deep "ho, ho, ho" like the laugh of an evil gnome. He was living in the cave of my stomach and using my mouth to get his laughs out.

Martin let go of me. He pulled Lisa's hands away from her face. "You have a nose."

"I do?" she asked hopefully.

"Yeah," said her boyfriend. "It's kinda short, but it's there."

"It's a beautiful nose," said Martin. He hugged Lisa. I didn't want Martin to fuse with her so I pulled him away and we walked on. "You did not hallucinate that," he scolded me. "You were just being mean."

"I don't like her."

"You can't be mean to anyone tripping. They're as vulnerable as you."

"Don't be mad at me, Martin. You're scaring me."

He stopped to hug me. "I love you."

"I love everybody."

He laughed. "That's the spirit."

We found a pay phone, and I called my mom. "Can I sleep over at Lisa's?" I asked.

"Well, Joanne, I don't know. I don't like these spur-of-the-moment plans. You don't even have your pajamas and toothbrush."

"Please, Mom."

"What's that racket?"

"It's the band, Mom. I'm at a dance. Lisa and I are having a groovy time."

"I didn't know you were that friendly with the Girardi girl."

"Please, Mom."

She knew what Lisa was, and all mothers want their girls to be popular. "Well, don't stay up talking and giggling all night."

"Thanks, Mom."

Then Martin and I did what you usually do at dances: we danced. Bright pink, purple, and orange lights swirled around us. Films of people kissing, trees swaying, and waves crashing played on the people between the projector and the walls. Strobe lights made the dancers' movements choppy and slow. Black lights bathed Martin's white T-shirt and teeth in a lavender glow. It was hard to tell the difference between the effects created by the light show and by the LSD. I didn't know where my own mind stopped and others' began. We seemed to all be in this together, of the same consciousness and organism, the pulsing colors our single heart beating to the rhythm of Roach.

Most everyone seemed to be having a good time, except one girl who kept screaming, "Let me out of my mind! Let me out of my mind!" She was bumming me out, and I wished she would shut up or go away. The dancers began to telescope out and crash inward. Chins elongated, then snapped to normal size. Legs and arms lengthened like spaghetti, then withdrew to their natural state. When it felt like my senses were on overload, I looked into Martin's face, which was serene and loving. Other times I closed my eyes to stop the girl from screaming or stuck my fingers in my ears to see nothing.

I felt no sense of past or future. Everything was in the now, like a piano performance. Time sped by. At two a.m. the hall began to empty out. The cops appeared, turning on the lights, unplugging sound equipment, and escorting people out. The let-me-out-of-my-mind girl was loaded into an ambulance, her hoarse voice still babbling.

Outside on the sidewalk I saw Lisa again. She had gotten separated from her boyfriend and was about to climb into a camper with some people I'd never seen.

"Oh, hi, Joanne." Her face, arms, and legs had been painted in swirls and paisleys of pink, orange, and purple Day-Glo paint. "We're going to the bridge. Do you want to come?"

The image of the Golden Gate Bridge terrified me. "No, I don't like the bridge." I took a step back, retreating into the safety of Martin's armpit.

Lisa smiled sweetly. Her best friend, Candy Lambert, had ridiculed me, and her ex-boyfriend, Kent Dougal, had humiliated me, and I suddenly realized I had blamed Lisa by association. She had even tried to be my friend. "Are you sure you don't want to come with us?" she asked. "It will be beautiful."

"I'm sure."

She hugged me good-bye, and some of her paint smeared onto my arm. Then she flashed a peace sign and disappeared into the camper.

Gus and the rest of the guys had already loaded their van. Martin and I sat on a pile of amps in the back. I couldn't see where we were going. I wished Lisa hadn't mentioned the bridge. I gripped Martin's arm so hard, he had to pry my fingers off him. "Easy, Joni. What's the matter?"

"Gus is going to drive off the bridge, I can feel it."

"You know we don't cross the bridge to get home."

"Stop! I have to get out! Right now!"

"Everything's cool, Joni. Gus! Pull over!"

As soon as we began walking along the marina, I felt better. The gently lapping water and the soft light of the streetlamps had a calming effect. I raised my chin to the sky. "Oh! Look at all those pretty lights!"

"The stars?"

"They look like neon lightbulbs that escaped from the Fillmore marquee and flew away." I jumped up and flung my arm as if I could catch one. "Do you think they'll ever come together and form one big, bright, blazing star?"

"No, Joni. They'll always stay separate and far away from each other."

One thing that troubled me about Martin was that I suspected he was not always up-front with me. Like, he was not up-front about who he spent his time with when he wasn't with me. Now he was not being up-front about the stars, so I decided to call him on it. "I know they do," I said, cautiously opening up a little trapdoor so that my consciousness could seep into his.

"Huh?"

"The stars do come together and make one big light during the day."

He surprised me by laughing. "That's just one star, Joni, our star, the sun."

"It's so much bigger because it's so much closer to us and those others are always far away?"

"Yep."

"You're far away like that, Martin."

"I'm not. I'm right here close."

"But you feel far away. You keep a distance. I wish I knew more about you. I wish we were closer."

He didn't answer.

"It's lonely on this trip. I wish you were tripping, too."

"It's better this way. Safer."

"I feel childish, like I can't take care of myself."

"You can't. That's why I'm here."

"We're not going near the bridge."

"Nope."

Before me was a whole string of stars that rose up, then swooped down and rose up again. I was about to tell Martin he was wrong, that the stars did come down to us, but then I realized why the tiny lights were in such neat, sloping lines. Horrified, I stopped. "You tricked me, Martin! We *are* going to the bridge!"

"You know there's a view of the bridge on the way to my house."

"Make it disappear."

"That's easy." He got on the other side of me to block my view. I felt a little better, but still uneasy. Martin pointed out details on a row of Victorians: the gables, the turrets, the bay windows, distracting me all the way to his house. I felt safer indoors. We climbed the stairs and entered his room.

"Do you think you can sleep?" he asked.

I didn't think so. "I can try." I lay on his bed, and he lay down next to me. The streetlight filtering in his window cast a thin black shadow that dropped into his back like an arrow. Some of the dance posters on his walls pictured Indians, and I thought of the Indians coming alive and shooting arrows into Martin's back and killing him. They couldn't come alive, though. I was looking at a harmless shadow. I was proud of that realization. I could be rational if I tried.

I stroked Martin's face and kissed him. I had that same sense of fusion; his lips were my lips and there was no boundary between us. It felt wonderful and I never wanted to stop. I was surprised when Martin pulled away. "Stop, Joni. I'm getting too turned on."

"What's wrong with that?"

"We aren't going to make love, not while you're tripping."

I ignored him and began kissing him again. I could seduce him with my kisses. He sprang from the bed, and I felt rejected. I sat up, my back against the wall, watching him pace. "Why are you so uptight all of a sudden? You've been wanting me to put out; here's your chance to get laid."

"Put out? What a horrible expression! If it's not making love, don't do it."

His words burned me with humiliation, and I found that LSD could be a sort of truth serum. It made me bold, allowing me to ask Martin questions I never would have dared to ask him without it. "I'll bet you've made love to lots of girls."

"Some."

On the beach at Angel Island he had said, "There's just you," but I had never allowed myself to believe him. "You have other girls, don't you?"

"What other girls?"

He seemed angry that I had figured this out. He seemed on the verge of lying to me, and I didn't want to force him into a lie. I held up a finger. "You're so very clever, aren't you, Martin? Acting like I mean something to you when, in fact, we're miles apart. But I do remember the time you first kissed me like you meant it. Do you? It was when we got into a fight about Morning Girl, and I said—"

He leaned over the bed and gently covered my mouth. "You said, 'Every child has the right to know who his father is.'" He took his hand away and sat beside me. "You were right on, my lady. I wish I knew who my father is."

"It's not Max?"

He shook his head. "When I was growing up, there was always a distance between him and me that I didn't understand. I always thought I was just an unlovable kid, but on our long drive out to California, Gus told me Max and Vivian weren't getting along when I was conceived. She carried on with a lot of men. Vivian wasn't much of a mom, always busy with her sculpture. Want to know who my real parent is? Gus. He saved me from drowning in a pond near our house when I was just two. Yep, I had an eight-year-old dad. Family life! It's totally fucked. That's why I'm never getting married and having kids."

"What if you fall in love with someone who wants to have kids with you?"

"Then I'd be a disappointment to her." He jumped up from the bed and reached for my hand. "I know what we can do."

"What?"

"Guess what's hiding in the basement?"

"The piano!"

I led the way, down the stairs and through the kitchen, but at the door to the basement, I stopped and turned sadly to Martin. "I can't go any further."

"Why not?"

"There's a door blocking my way."

"Turn the knob."

"Oh." I was amazed that the solution to my problem was so easy.

The piano was out of tune, and the warbling of the dissonant harmonies fighting each other made me feel like there were exotic birds squawking in my brain. As I pressed the keys, the sound seemed to come from my fingers rather than the piano. The piano played legato; it played staccato. My fingers pattered like rain on the keys.

I was aware that others were sleeping in the house, so I played softly. There was a book of Scott Joplin rags on the piano, and I opened it and began to sight-read "The Strenuous Life." When I got to the end of the second page, I stopped and looked at Martin, who was sitting on the sofa. "There's no more music," I said sadly.

"Turn the page."

Another obstacle easily overcome. Was that really who I was? Someone who was so easily discouraged?

I played some more in the Joplin book. I played everything I knew by heart, even little parts of pieces I had memorized long ago and hadn't thought of for years. It was fun to play the piano like this, just playing, not practicing, not getting ready for some dreaded date in the future. I thought about the expression "play the piano." I wondered if I could play better if I worked less.

I sat staring at the keys, trying to think of something else to play. Behind me, Martin was snoring softly. I wasn't at all sleepy; I wasn't hungry. I had nothing to do and no one to talk to. The dawning light was seeping through the windows, so I decided to go home.

I slipped out of Martin's house, crossed the street, and waited a few minutes for the trolley. It was cold. I reached in my car coat pockets for my cap and mittens. I stomped my feet, and then I began to put one in front of the other. I reached the Golden Gate Bridge and stepped out onto it, just to prove to myself I was no longer afraid. I walked through the Presidio, down Lincoln Way, and along the Great Highway, past the Sutro Baths, Cliff House, and Seal Rocks. The walking seemed effortless, like the road was as springy as the soles of my red Keds.

I was coming down. It wasn't a crash landing into hard, cold reality like I'd dreaded, but more like a gentle descent by parachute. Everything in the world was more beautiful than when I had left on my trip: the sky, the seagulls, the wind, the water, my life.

I had never hiked the entire length of Golden Gate Park, but I was going to do it that Sunday morning. I turned in at the windmill and kept walking, past Spreckels Lake and the Japanese Tea Garden. Lying on the walkway near the de Young Museum was a perfect long-stemmed rose, something that had not grown in the park in this season. A gift for me. I picked it up and carried it with me, past the band concourse and Hippie Hill.

Soon I had crossed Stanyan and was walking up Frederick Street, home from my trip. I had survived. I would be a better person, I decided, good to Lisa and my parents, even Dan. I opened our gate, ran up our driveway, and bounded through the back door into the kitchen.

Both my parents were waiting for me at the table. They didn't look happy.

My mother snatched the rose I was holding and began thrashing my head with it. I tucked my face into the crook of my elbow, even though it didn't hurt. The petals fluttering to the floor made me sad. When my mother was done, my beautiful rose was nothing but a stem, which she threw on the floor. I picked it up.

"You ungrateful brat!" she screamed. "You had us up all night worried sick."

"I told you I was spending the night at Lisa's."

Dad folded his newspaper. "Lisa didn't come home last night, Joanne. Leo Girardi called here looking for her."

"But we were together at the dance and—"

"The dance got out at eleven," said Mom. "Where have you been all this time?"

I sat at my place at the table and set the rose stem carefully before me. A single tear slid down my cheek. "The dance got out at two a.m. Me and Lisa went to the Fillmore. I knew it was too late to come home so I stayed at some friends' house."

"What friends?" asked Mom.

I shrugged. "Just some people I met around the neighborhood."

"Hippies?" asked Mom.

"Well...yeah."

"My God! Were you raped?"

"No, Mom."

"Was Lisa with you?" asked Dad.

"Uh...no. I saw her get into a camper with a bunch of people she met at the Fillmore."

"Ah, hell. Leo said she's been running wild," said Dad.

"And our daughter hasn't been?" asked Mom.

"She's not a drug addict like the Girardi girl!" Dad rose from his chair. "I better call Leo. Let him know what we know. You're not lying to us now, Joanne?"

"No, Dad!"

When he left the kitchen to make the call, Mom glared at me and shook her head. "I don't even know you anymore, Joanne. You've always been the difficult child to raise, but I never thought it would come to this, staying out all night at the age of sixteen."

"I'm sorry, Mom. The Purple Cockroach is my favorite band. They were playing at the Fillmore, and I wanted to hear them. If I asked you, you wouldn't let me go."

The doorbell rang. I could hear Dad hanging up and going to answer it.

"Going into the Negro slum, hanging around with hopped-up

hippies? No mother in her right mind would allow her daughter to do that!"

"You never let me do anything! If I waited for your permission, I'd never go anywhere."

Dad appeared at the kitchen entrance. "Lisa still hasn't come home. Leo's calling the police," he reported, obviously shaken. "There's someone here to see you, Joanne." He stepped aside, and there was Martin! He looked so out of place in my mother's rooster decor, I thought I was still tripping. He wore clean Levi's and a denim shirt, tucked in. His hair was washed and brushed back in a neat ponytail. I wanted to scream, "Run, run! My parents are so mad they'll kill you!"

Martin extended his hand to my mother, and she reluctantly shook it. "Hello, Mrs. Donnelly. I'm Martin. Joanne spent the night at our house, and when I woke up, I found out she was gone. I was worried about her, so I just came over to see she got home okay."

"She's here," Mom said flatly. "Have a seat. Would you like some coffee?"

"I don't do caffeine. Do you have any herbal tea?"

"No, we don't have any herbal tea," said Dad.

"Just a cup of hot water, then," said Martin.

"Plain hot water?" Mom exclaimed.

"Water from the tap would be fine," said Martin.

Mom poured a glass of water and handed it to him. "Do your parents let you stay out all night?"

"Um...well, I live with my older brother, and he uh..."

"Lets you do pretty much what you want," said Mom. "Do you think we should let Joanne do whatever she wants?"

"Well, she has pretty good judgment."

"You think staying out all night is good judgment?" asked Dad.

"No, that wasn't," said Martin. "I should have taken her home at two, when the dance ended, but it was late and—"

"Are you having sexual intercourse with our daughter?" roared Dad, leaning over Martin, his hands on his hips.

"No!" Martin raised both palms. "No," he repeated softly.

"But you have been seeing each other for quite a while," said Mom.

"No!" I exclaimed.

"Yes," said Martin. "Long enough for me to drop by and meet the family."

"And what do you do together?" Mom asked.

"We talk a lot," said Martin.

"And walk a lot," I added.

"And drink tea," said Martin.

"Herbal tea?" Dad clarified disdainfully.

"Right," said Martin, "with honey. And sometimes we play music together. Last night we went dancing."

"Joanne is forbidden to attend the Fillmore or the Avalon dances ever again!" said Mom. "Are we clear about that?"

"Right," said Martin. "I won't take her there again."

"What are your intentions toward our daughter?" asked Dad.

"Well . . ." Martin rubbed his chin. "I was just going to ask her if she wanted to go down to Tracy's for a donut."

"You better run along to Tracy's Donuts on your own," said Mom. "I was just about to ground Joanne for life."

"Oh. Okay. Well . . ." Martin slowly stood. "It was nice to meet you, Mr. and Mrs. Donnelly. Thanks for the water." He turned and gave me one of his beautiful smiles. I wanted to kick him for coming to my house. "Bye, Joni. Glad you made it home okay."

"Not everyone did," said Dad. He showed Martin out the back door. My parents and I were silent, listening to the gravel crunch beneath Martin's boots as he passed under the kitchen window.

When we heard the gate clink shut, Mom started yelling again. "What are we going to do about this, Dick? What sort of man wears a ponytail?"

"I don't know," said Dad. "But a fella who comes around to my front door, looks me in the eye, and inquires about the safety of my daughter is the sort of man I like."

Mom flapped her arms. "It's okay with you that your daughter dates a hippie?"

"I'll let you handle this one, Mother." Dad picked up his newspaper and shuffled into the den.

Sitting at the kitchen table with all the roosters looking on, I knew I was in for a serious interrogation. I was going to try to be honest with my mother, something I hadn't had much practice with.

"Do you and Martin smoke marijuana together?"

I winced. "A couple of times."

Mom sighed deeply. "I thought so. I read a survey where sixty-two percent of you kids have tried it, so I knew you'd be one of them."

"I don't really like it, Mom. It makes me confused, and I'd rather think straight. You know I have a hard time remembering my music as it is. I don't know how musicians play stoned. Even in rock you've got to remember chord changes and lyrics."

"Does Martin go to school?"

"No."

"Does he have a job?"

"Sorta. He works for his brother sometimes."

"Doing what?"

"Setting up his rock band."

"Oh, brother. He's all wrong for you, Joanne, but I can tell by the way you look at each other that no matter what Dad and I say or do, you'll find a way to keep seeing him. Don't get pregnant, Joanne. It would ruin your life if you married him."

"Mom! I'm too young to be looking for a husband."

"Exactly what your sister said. She barely lasted a year at Cal before she got one. Don't get me wrong. You know we love Jerry, but it would have been nice if someone in this family had actually graduated from college, and Denise was the one who could actually do it."

"Thanks a lot."

"Well, Joanne, I honestly don't have much hope for you. Smoking marijuana and playing the guitar and running after hippies, I imagine you'll soon be one yourself."

I swallowed hard. I tried not to show that she had succeeded in hurting my feelings. "Can I go to Tracy's now?"

"I'd better let you. If I sent you to your room you'd leap out of the second-story window to chase after that hippie."

When I got to Tracy's, Martin had my favorite donut, a custard-filled, chocolate-iced Bismark, waiting for me. "What made you think I was coming?"

"Your parents seem to be reasonable folks."

"Martin! Are you crazy?"

He laughed. "We've been sneaking around long enough. It's bad karma the way you lie to your parents because of me."

"They could've forbidden me to see you ever again."

"I thought of that. But you'd find a way."

"That's what my mom figured." I scarfed down my donut.

Martin reached across the table with a napkin to wipe the chocolate from my mouth. "Why'd you take off without telling me?" he asked softly.

"You were asleep, and I was wide awake."

"How do you feel now?"

"Good. Thoughtful. I don't know if I'll ever want to drop acid again. It's going to take me about ten years to sort this trip out."

"I knew you were a quick learner." His smiling eyes grew soft and deep. "You said something last night that made me sad."

It was impossible to remember everything I had rattled on about. "What?"

"What makes you think I have other girls?"

I felt myself blush. "Well, we don't . . . you know, and Rena told me that once guys start having sex they have to have it, and now everyone is into free love, and—"

"You're doing it again, Joni. Stereotyping me. Can't you think of me as my own person?"

"I'm sorry. I—"

"There's nobody but you, got that, lady? I'll let you know when that changes."

"Not *if,* but *when.*"

"I warned you from the start. I'm a rolling stone."

"I know." I looked down at my hands. There was chocolate icing stuck under my thumbnail.

"And you've got big plans. Juilliard. Carnegie Hall."

I knew all this, and Martin was right in thinking I occasionally needed to be reminded. I noticed a smear of pink Day-Glo paint on my arm and had to think hard where it came from. "Where do you think Lisa is?"

He lifted one shoulder and dropped it. "Sleeping it off wherever that camper took her."

"She was going to the bridge."

# CHAPTER
# SIXTEEN

April Fools' Day I really was sick, no joke. I'd been throwing up all night and I had a fever. Still, Mom was convinced I was faking. It was her bridge day—Thelma was hosting—and Mom accused me of planning to cut school to meet Martin in the park or somewhere as soon as she left the house. That was actually a pretty good idea. I would have to try it someday when I felt better.

All morning, between fits of sleep, I was aware of Snoopy purring and kneading my pillow. I thought, Now I'm supposed to be in geometry, now world history, now orchestra. It was weird to think of the school day going on without me. Around eleven o'clock I heard Mom taking a shower, and when she checked on me just before leaving, I pretended to be asleep. A little while later I felt well enough to sit up in bed and finish the letter to Jimmy I'd started the previous evening. I'd been writing to him every two weeks or so, nothing personal, just the stuff he'd asked me to write about. He wrote back a couple of times, but not with news of the war; he liked to reminisce about home and make plans for when he returned, including a fishing trip to Clear Lake with Dan.

Just as I was sealing the envelope, I heard the back door close. Mom, no doubt, had rushed home to check on me. I heard footsteps on the stairs, and then Denise burst into the room.

"What are you doing here?" we said in unison.

"I've got the flu," I said.

"Oh, give it to me so I can take the rest of the week off!"

"Aren't you supposed to be at work right now?"

Denise sank heavily onto her bed. "Yeah. I went to lunch, then found I just couldn't face Mr. Marlowe and his roaming hands."

My eyes popped.

"Now when he stands behind me, he puts his hands on my breasts. He says it helps him think."

"That's horrible! There should be a law against it."

"There isn't." She seemed resigned to the situation, when the Denise I once knew would be sprinting around the desk yelling, "Hands off!"

"You should tell Jerry."

"Why would he care? He's got his life arranged just the way he wants it. Did you hear the news yesterday? LBJ has decided not to run for reelection. That's just icing on the cake. Now it seems Jerry will even get the president he wants—Gene McCarthy."

"Maxine wants Bobby Kennedy."

Denise shrugged. "It makes me tired to talk about politics. I just came over here to sit in this little pink room and—I don't know—find myself." She picked up a framed picture from her senior prom. "Oh, here I am. Look at me! I was so young and pretty then."

"That was only two years ago, Den. You're still young and pretty."

She rubbed her cheek. "I feel like an old hag. All used up." She lifted a volume of the complete novels of Jane Austen onto her lap. "And here I am. My favorite is *Sense and Sensibility*. I felt I was both of them. Ah! My little book of poems." She flipped through a cloth-covered notebook, pausing to read here and there. "God! All bad imitations of Rod McKuen. Still, they're mine. I wrote them."

I tapped a huge art history textbook lying horizontally in the bookcase. "There's you again."

"Ah, no, Jo, not really. I only declared art history because I knew Cal had quotas in various majors and I had a better chance of getting in. I figured I'd switch to English later."

"You should go back to college."

"Jerry and I fight about it all the time. He says I have penis envy."

It took me a few seconds to understand what she was talking about. "Wait, I don't get it. Jerry thinks you wish you had one?"

"Uh-huh. Freud talks about it all the time. He says that's usually why women are so unhappy."

"Yew, that's sickening! Why would a girl want a...an *elephant trunk* hanging off her body?"

Denise reeled with laughter. "Oh, Jo, you're so funny!"

"Seriously. Why would you need a *thing* to go to college? Talk to Maxine. You need to be liberated."

"Jerry has already liberated me quite enough. We now have an open marriage. He calls it group sex, like group therapy, like it's all clinical and normal, but it's just a filthy orgy."

I stared back at her.

"I'm talking to the wrong person about this. Don't tell Mom. I want her to go to her grave without knowing people do such things."

"She's not that out of it."

"I don't want her to know her daughter does such things."

"How is that liberation if you don't like it? You don't have to go to ogres if you don't want to."

"Christ, Joanne, it's *orgies*. Either I go or risk losing my husband to some slut who's there on her own."

I kicked off the blankets and leaped out of bed. "That does it. I'm liberating you myself! Take off your bra."

Denise looked up from her book of poems. It seemed she had finally found one she sort of liked. "What?"

"Go on. Take off your bra. Here's one of mine. Come on, we're burning them!"

Denise let out a hoot and slapped her knee. "I'm in!"

I rushed down the stairs to fetch matches from the kitchen. Soon Denise bounded down after me, a bit jiggly, waving her bra. I threw my car coat over my pajamas, and we burst through the French doors onto the patio. I dropped my bra into the brick barbecue pit, while Denise dangled hers over it.

"This is silly, really," she said.

I snatched her bra from her hand and threw it down. I doused both bras with lighter fluid and dropped a match over them before Denise could change her mind. The elastic curled and sputtered and turned black. It stank. I watched the roaring flame in Denise's pupils. She looked beautiful.

When our bras were nothing but ash, Dan came loping into the backyard, waving a packet of papers. "I did it! I enlisted in the marines!"

"What about college?" asked Denise.

Dan batted the air. "I haven't been going to class since January. I probably flunked out by now. I took all the tests at the recruiting office today: written, practical application, physical. I was the best recruit in push-ups! I knew I would be!"

Denise and I stared at each other across the remains of our smoldering bras. "Congratulations," she said flatly.

"Thanks," said Dan. He hit the deck and pumped out a few push-ups. He collapsed onto his belly and craned his neck to look up at us. "Yew, what's that *smell*?"

"We're having a wienie roast," I said. "Hey, you know what it's called when you're at a party and someone has a hot dog and you don't? Wienie envy!"

Denise's laugh came out like a snort.

After Dan ran into the house, I said, "He's been dying for a chance to get himself killed, and now he's got it."

"Maybe not. Jerry is campaigning for Gene, the peace candidate."

"Maxine is campaigning for Bobby, the peace candidate. I hope they don't cancel each other out."

Denise sighed. "Guess I better go. Jerry will be expecting dinner, and I have to stop at Macy's on the way home to shop for a new bra."

"Denise!"

"Are you kidding me, Jo? If I went around like this, in a couple of months I'd have nothing but a pair of string beans!"

I clasped my hand against my breasts. "And it does sorta hurt."

"Yeah, and hairy legs and pits like Maxine's are just plain gross!"

I had failed to liberate Denise, but at least I had cheered her up some.


Three days later Martin Luther King, Jr., was gunned down outside his motel room in Memphis, and riots erupted in over a hundred cities. Dan made a show of propping his hunting rifle against our front door, his BB gun at the back door, and a machete at the French doors in case all-out war broke out between white and black. I couldn't tell if he was joking or not.

The next day my parents kept me home from school. Our attention was focused to the north, toward our nearest Negro neighbors, in the Fillmore District. That day we could hear the shattering glass as every storefront on Haight Street was broken. As far as I knew, that was the worst of it. There were no deaths, at least not on our side of the bay. On Saturday, Black Panther Bobby Hutton was shot in a gun battle with the Oakland Police.

"Hell, what *do* they want?" asked Dan.

In an article in the *Oakland Tribune,* the Panthers made their demands clear in their Ten-Point Program. It included freedom, employment, housing, education, health care, and the end of police brutality and wars of aggression.

I read it aloud to my family at the kitchen table. "Sounds like they want the same as what everyone wants."

# CHAPTER
## SEVENTEEN

When I got home from school the first Monday in June, I found Maxine in the kitchen with Mom, no bridge party in sight.

"I'm just not in favor of it," said Mom.

"Of what?" I asked, nosing in.

"Joanne, what are you doing in school tomorrow?" Maxine asked.

"Nothing." It really was nothing. Instruction was done. In most of my classes we'd be applying sandpaper to the edges of textbooks.

"How would you like to meet the next president of the United States?" Maxine gushed.

"Far out."

"I'm just not in favor of it," said Mom, and she and Maxine argued some more. While Mom could wear Dad down in two minutes flat on just about any subject, she'd met her match in Maxine.

The next morning, Maxine's 1958 Buick Riviera, about the length of a city block, rolled up to our curb to whisk me and my overnight case off to the Ambassador Hotel in Los Angeles, campaign headquarters for Robert F. Kennedy. It was the day of the California primary election, and "Bobby" was favored to win the Democratic Party nomination. We were going to be witnesses to the historic event of his victory speech.

It was a fine day to be zooming down Highway 101, the cool morning breeze catching my hair through the open window. I'd only been to L.A. once, to Disneyland when I was eight, and now being Maxine's sidekick felt like a real adult adventure. She and I talked and laughed together like we were girls of the same age. I found myself going on and on about Martin.

"It sounds like this boy is a real soul mate for you."

"Yeah, but I don't know how long it will last."

"So what? It's great for now. Now is the time in your life when you should be experiencing all sorts of relationships. You don't have to marry a guy just because he's right for you now. I envy you girls today. You have all sorts of freedoms I never experienced when I was your age. I didn't have sex before I was married, and neither did any of the girls I knew. We were all terrified of getting pregnant and then being forced into the home for unwed mothers and having our babies raised by strangers. You are using the Pill, aren't you, Joanne, or some other method of birth control?"

"Uh, I don't . . . we don't sleep together."

"Well, when the time comes, let me know, and I'll make the appointment and come with you."

I'd already thought about this on my own. I had actually gone with Denise for her gynecology appointment, so I knew the doctor's name and where his office was. "Thanks, Maxine. I appreciate that."

"You're welcome, Joanne. You know I love your mother, but she's so old-fashioned about these things."

In fact, Mom's main objection to my going to L.A. with Maxine was that she assumed Quentin would be with us, and Mom did not approve of an unmarried couple sharing a hotel room. "I thought Quentin was coming."

"Oh, no. I don't see much of him lately. He has a lover now, and he usually stays over at his house."

"Oh," I said. "Oh!"

"You do know about homosexuals, don't you, Joanne?"

"Yeah, but . . ." I had to smile. "Mom and the bridge ladies thought Quentin was your boyfriend."

Maxine raised her chin and emitted a hoot. "That explains a lot! Don't they think he's a little young for me?" She laughed again. "Oh, yes, I imagine they do! And I thought all their whispering behind my back was just about my not wearing a bra. Ha! No, Joanne. My lover is much more mature than Quentin, and I'd never bring him around those gossipmongers. I don't see him that much, anyway, because he's married, but I've decided that's the way I like it."

Maxine then went on about *her* boyfriend, which was a little boring, until she got around to mentioning that she'd met him at Denise's wedding, and that he had a little boy and a rather demanding teenage daughter who was trying to launch a career in the theater. Rena. It was a confusing world I lived in, with some relationships so close, it seemed they were tied in knots.

That night Maxine had tears running down her face when Bobby Kennedy made his victory speech to his adoring public. Those tears turned to a different sort later on, when shots rang out from the hotel kitchen, which Kennedy was cutting through. He was pronounced dead shortly after midnight.

As Maxine wove her big Buick through morning traffic on our way home, she was crying such torrents I was afraid she would run off the road. When we pulled up to her house, there was a person curled up on her porch beneath the tarp she used to cover her lawn furniture in winter.

"Quentin, is that you?" She shook what appeared to be a shoulder, and up popped Denise's head.

Inside, we made breakfast as we told Denise about the assassination. When we sat down to eat, Denise told us her story. "Mr. Marlowe asked me to work late, with just him and me in the building, and the girls around the office had warned me what that meant. I refused him, and when he threatened to fire me, I quit! I'd rather starve than get laid by that creep."

"Wait a minute," I said. "I thought you once said the office girls warned you that if you *did* have sex with him, he'd fire you. Isn't that what happened to the girl you replaced?"

"Oh, yeah, huh?" Denise shrugged. "I guess it works both ways. Anyway, when I walked out on Mr. Marlowe, I realized

I didn't want to go home, either. I've left Jerry!" Her splotched, angry face spurted fresh tears. "I still love him, but there's just too many things wrong with our marriage. Can I stay with you, Maxine? Just until I get another job and a ... a place of my own."

"Of course you can, dear," said Maxine, handing her one Kleenex after another. "But there will be conditions."

"I can keep house for you."

"That isn't it. I want you to resist running back to Jerry right away. I want you to learn to stand on your own two feet."

"O ... kay," Denise whimpered. "It will be hard."

"We'll just keep it quiet where you're staying for the time being. Joanne, don't tell your parents just so they can send Jerry over here. Denise, how good are you at persuasive writing?"

"I can do it. I used to write a column for my high school newspaper."

"Good. Dry your eyes, Denise, and get cleaned up while I run Joanne home. After that, we'll go over to Gene McCarthy's headquarters and introduce ourselves. We're got a new candidate to work for."

Maxine didn't take the time to come in when she dropped me off. I found Mom in the kitchen making lunch for Dan and Dad, who was in his business suit, in the middle of his rounds. Dan was hunched over a letter he had received in the mail, his eyes squinted like he was having difficulty reading it.

"Maxine isn't stopping in?" Mom asked me.

"She's really torn up."

"It's tragic," said Mom. "That handsome young man, gunned down not five years after his brother. My heart goes out to those Kennedys."

"I just don't get it," said Dan, still staring at his letter. "I thought I was doing good on the test."

"Maybe you were too slow putting the rifle together," said Dad, "or you left out some parts."

"What's going on?" I asked.

Vulnerability clouded Dan's eyes as he peered at me over his letter. "The marines rejected me. I flunked the practical applications test."

He always was a klutz with mechanical things, but I never knew he was this bad. "I'm sorry, Dan. I know that was your dream."

Dan ripped his letter to shreds. "Screw it! If I'm not good enough for the marines, to hell with the army! Guess I'm not going to Nam after all. Jimmy will be coming home soon, anyways, and we can pal around like old times. I might as well go back to college and become a business guy like you, Dad."

"I don't think it works that way, son," Dad said quietly. "Your student deferment is long gone. I expect you'll be hearing from your draft board soon."

That evening my parents were about to leave for dinner and dancing and I was putting water on to boil hot dogs, when Jerry came through the back door looking for Denise.

"You should have called before coming all this way," said Mom. "She must be working late." She reached up and tried to smooth Jerry's wrinkled shirt. "We have to run, dear. Joanne, offer Jerry a wiener."

"Want a wiener, Wienerfield?"

"No," he said flatly, flinging himself into a kitchen chair. After my parents left, he asked, "Where is she?"

"I . . . don't know." The water began to boil, and I dropped two hot dogs into it. I was glad I had something to do to avoid his steely glare.

"You do, too. She didn't come home last night, and when I went over to Marlowe Advertising Agency the girl at the front desk said she no longer worked there. She wouldn't give me any more information. 'Fess up, Beethoven. Where's Denise?"

"I know, but I'm not telling."

He rubbed his hands through his hair. "I don't have time for her little games, and I'm hungry!"

"I'll make you a hot dog."

"I don't want a damn hot dog. I want my wife!" He slammed

his fist down and shouted toward the living room. "Denise! Don't be so damn immature! Come out of hiding and let's go home."

"You don't get it, do you? She's left you. She can't stand those ogres."

Jerry sneered. "You mean those little monsters that live under a bridge and eat the Billy Goats Gruff?"

I blushed, but I didn't back down. "You know what I mean. It's disgusting!"

He looked sheepish. "Did she tell your parents about that?"

"Are you dead yet? No, you aren't. Dan has been dying to shoot someone, and he wouldn't even care you're not a gook, since this comes down to the family's honor."

Jerry groaned. "It was just a little experiment."

"Experiment! You think your marriage is one of those white rats they keep in the psych department at Cal?"

"I just wanted to help her loosen up some."

"She was loose until you laid all that dumb Freud shit on her. Can't you just love each other and let it go at that?"

"If I want advice on my sex life from a fifteen-year-old virgin, I'll ask for it, thank you very much."

"Sixteen. And she doesn't need a...a...*dick* to go to college."

"*What?* Oh. Penis envy. You shouldn't talk about stuff you know nothing about, Beethoven."

I got up, turned off the stove, nestled my two hot dogs in buns already spread with mustard, poured a glass of milk, and brought my food over to the table.

Jerry's eyes grew wide as I chomped down on my first delicious bite. "I wish I knew how to make hot dogs."

I got up, dumped the water out of the pan, and placed it in his hand. He stared at it like it was a foreign object he'd never seen. "Bring it over to the sink, Whinerfield. Fill it about half full with water and set it on the stove."

After he'd followed those directions, he asked, "Which knob do I turn?"

"That one, on high. Good. Now when the water starts to boil, plop the dogs in, and take them out in three minutes."

"That's it?"

"You just uncovered one of the great mysteries of human existence. I don't even know why you bother studying Freud. Maxine says he's a stupid old fuddy-duddy who hates women."

"So now we're getting to the bottom of this. That fag hag has been brainwashing Denise with all her women's lib shit. The bull dyke bitch!"

"You think calling Maxine disgusting names is going to get your wife back?"

"I'm sorry," he said grudgingly. "Tell Denise to come home, and we'll talk things out. We can go back to a monogamous marriage. I'm fine with that."

"It's not going to be that easy. Denise hasn't been happy for a long time."

He groaned. "Hell! I'll have to move back in with my aunt. And then she'll call my parents, and then they'll give me the told-you-so lecture."

"Don't give up so easily, Jerry Whinerfield."

"I can't batch it. How would I feed myself?"

"You already know how to make hot dogs. How good are you with peanut butter?"

"Very funny."

"Take off your shirt." I set up the ironing board and plugged in the iron.

"Gee, thanks, Beethoven. Could you iron about six more? Denise has sorta fallen behind."

"You're gonna do it. Look, first you have to check to see if the iron is hot enough. Lick your finger like this, then touch it to the iron real quick." My wet finger went *hiss.* "Hear that? It's ready. Now you try."

Jerry looked unsure, but he licked his finger and applied it to the iron. "Yeow!"

"I said touch it, not lay on it for a half hour. Your water's ready. Dump the hot dogs in."

He put in four. I guessed he really was hungry. "Ouch!" He rubbed his hand.

I laughed. "You baby."

"Boiling water splashed up and scalded my hand! I'm not cut out for women's work!"

"Gimme that shirt. Look, you always do the collar first. Lay it flat like so, squirt it with water. The trick is to keep the iron moving so you don't scorch the material. Here, you try." I stepped away, and Jerry took up the iron and ran it gingerly across the collar. "Press harder. Keep it moving! Good. Cuffs come next. If you expect to get your wife back, I'm going to have to liberate you."

# CHAPTER
# EIGHTEEN

At the end of Suyu Li's senior recital, I rose to my feet, my hands stinging from how hard I'd clapped. She had performed brilliantly a very difficult program, including Beethoven's *"Hammerklavier"* and Debussy's *Estampes*. I might never make it to Carnegie Hall, but Suyu was sure to, and I promised myself I would make the trip to New York to applaud for her when she performed there.

A couple of days later, as I sat in the orchestra at our high school's graduation, I clapped some more as Suyu's name was announced over and over for awards and scholarships. I wanted to congratulate her afterward, but in the confusion of the graduates tossing their mortarboards like Frisbees and dashing to the end of the stadium to pick up their diplomas, I never found her. The class of 1968 had graduated, and that meant I was a senior.

Saturday morning, Mr. Li pulled up in front of our house in his delivery truck. Mom spied on him from behind the lace curtains at the bay window. "What's that Chinaman doing? He knows we always pick up our own dry cleaning."

Suyu got out of the passenger side of the truck and opened our gate for her dad. He was carrying what seemed to be a very heavy wooden crate, which did not look like dry cleaning. Suyu followed him with a cardboard box. Mr. Li set his load on the porch, rang the doorbell, and left. His truck putted away as I answered the door.

"Suyu! What's all this?"

"A present for you, Joanne." She set the box she was carrying in our foyer, and together we lugged in the crate. "I thought you would be the best person to inherit all my music. I know you will appreciate Dr. Harold's notes."

"You're getting all new music for college?"

She smiled. "No, no. I won't be needing it anymore. I've quit the piano!"

My jaw dropped. "You . . . you can't quit! Oh, wow, what's Dr. Harold going to say?"

"He's known for a long time."

"And he's going to *let* you?"

She laughed. "Joanne, you're so funny!"

"I don't get it! Your recital was fantastic! You're the best!"

"I'm pretty good, but there's lots of pianists better than me. It's practically impossible to make a good living as a musician. I'm done with being poor, and my parents deserve an easy retirement. I'll see to that."

"But the piano is your life."

"It was a nice hobby, Joanne, but it was never my life."

"What will you do?"

"I got a full scholarship to MIT. I'm going to build computers! They're the wave of the future. One of these days everybody will have one in their house, like TV."

I thought of the huge computer Jerry had showed me in the Cal psych department; it filled an entire wall. "People are going to have computer rooms in their houses?"

"Oh, no. Already computers are small enough to set on a desk."

"But what for?"

"All sorts of things. To calculate, store data, produce documents, communicate."

"Won't there be any telephones in the future?"

"Oh, yes! And when you answer, the person calling will see you, like a little movie."

I wasn't so sure I wanted people to see me in my pajamas or with my hair all messed up. "Will you *have* to be seen?" I asked.

"I don't know how it's all going to work, Joanne, but it will be exciting to find out. Even cars will be different. By the year 2000, there won't be any wheels on them. They'll just hover about two inches off the ground!"

I wasn't impressed. How could anyone, especially Suyu, plan a future without Beethoven? I glanced down at the volumes of music at my feet. "Won't you want to sit down and play every once in a while?"

She wrinkled her nose. "Without practicing? It would only be frustrating. I have a recording of my senior recital. I'm happy with that. And now whenever I come to any big problem in computers, I'll think, I can solve it. I played my senior recital, and that's the hardest thing I'll ever do."

Suyu chatted on, but I was having a hard time paying attention. Two treasure troves lay at my feet, and my fingers itched to dig in. As soon as she left, I dove for her Beethoven sonatas. With shaking hands, I flipped to the *"Pathétique."* What? Dr. Harold had to remind Suyu to play staccato here, and count the rests there, and voice the melody here? Those were just the same things he'd told me! Suyu had had to *learn* this stuff just like me!

That summer the influx of hippies that filled Haight-Ashbury was not as great as it had been in the Summer of Love. Even hippies discouraged hippies from coming, like the ad in the Oracle that read, "Kansas City needs you. Start your own revolution in your own town." The Diggers had stopped serving free meals in the Panhandle long ago, and with noise ordinances in effect, there were fewer free outdoor concerts. The cops routinely canvassed the neighborhood, searching for runaways and shipping them home. Photos of missing teens were taped on lampposts and in storefronts. By now Lisa Girardi's portrait was faded and cracked. Her parents had hired a private eye without results; she had slipped away from the Fillmore without a trace. Hundreds of times I thought about hugging Lisa that February night. If only I had held on to her long enough for that camper to drive away without her.

I hardly saw anything of Rena. She was performing in summer stock in Santa Maria. Martin tried to come over a few times, but there were rules. He was banned from our house when my parents weren't home, and he was not allowed in my room ever. When we watched TV in the den, there was no touching. That last restraint wasn't exactly a rule, but it felt like one.

We preferred to meet at the coffee shops on Haight Street, usually the Tangerine Kangaroo. Once when Martin was there playing his guitar and singing, he invited me to join him onstage. We sang in harmony, him taking the top part. Coins and a few dollar bills were dropped into his open guitar case.

"I'm hungry. You want anything?"

I shook my head. "I had lunch at home."

"Cool. You can take over." He set his guitar in my lap.

"Martin, no!" I whispered. "I can't do this by myself."

He stooped to collect the money in his case before going to order at the counter. "You're a pianist! This is much easier than Beethoven."

He was right about that. I launched into "Little Boxes." Then I played "Leaving on a Jet Plane" and "Where Have All the Flowers Gone?" A group of tourists happened in, and were generous in their donations to Martin's case. As I was scooping out the money, Martin said, "You made a killing. You can donate some to the Free Clinic."

"Not a chance. This is the first money I've made as a professional musician, and I'm keeping every cent of it."

"Whoa, Joni, I didn't know you were such a capitalist pig," said Martin, but he was laughing.

I tried to get him interested in rehearsing together. "We could be like Simon and Garfunkel."

"That's two guys."

"Okay, then. Peter, Paul, and Mary, without Paul. Or Peter."

Martin just shook his head. "Spontaneous is better. Rehearsing would take all the fun out of it. Soon we'd be at each other's throats like Gus and the guys in Roach."

Everybody worked to get Eugene McCarthy nominated as the Democratic antiwar candidate. Martin was one of the many hippies who trimmed his hair in order to campaign door to door as part of the "get clean for Gene" effort. Maxine had gotten Denise a secretarial position in the women's studies department at Cal, and Denise had applied to a scholarship program that sponsored "returning women students." In her spare time, she wrote editorials promoting McCarthy, which appeared in the *Oracle*, the *Berkeley Barb*, and other publications under the byline D. Donnelly.

Our efforts were wasted. In August, amid a violent clash between ten thousand protesters and 23,000 Chicago policemen and National Guardsmen, the 1968 Democratic National Convention named Vice-President Hubert Humphrey its party's candidate. Humphrey seemed unclear about what he would do about the war. Whatever he decided, it was probably be too late for Dan. He'd been drafted and was expected to be deployed in early December.

Denise and Jerry kept their separation private to avoid having their parents interfering in their affairs. I was almost sure Mom was on to them because it seemed so obvious. Denise and Jerry had invited us to dinner at least once a month, and those invitations had stopped. If Denise or Jerry accepted an invitation for both of them from Mom, Denise came alone and made an excuse for Jerry, or vice versa, or they both canceled at the last moment.

Jerry had to get a part-time job at the copy shop to cover his rent. It was a good thing I had taught him to make hot dogs, because that was about the only meat he could afford. I went over to Berkeley about once a week to continue his liberation lessons: cooking, laundering, vacuuming, waxing, and window washing.

His biggest obstacle was scouring out a gunky frying pan. As soon as he approached it, he started gagging. Wimpfield! I had to buy him a Teflon pan with my own money.

At the end of August, Jerry got the nerve to invite Denise to dinner. I came over in the afternoon to supervise as he cleaned the apartment and made the meat loaf, baked potatoes, and tossed green salad. Everything was ready on time. Ten minutes ticked by, and no Denise.

"Is this her game? Getting me all excited about seeing her, then not showing up?"

"She'll be here."

Jerry flipped through an old *Berkeley Barb* and pointed to an editorial by D. Donnelly. "Do you read this guy? He's pretty good."

I looked over to what he was pointing at. "That's Denise."

He laughed out loud.

"It is. I thought you knew."

Jerry read over the article, smiling proudly. "She can write, that's for damn sure. D. Donnelly, for God's sake. Has she gone back to her maiden name legally?"

"She wasn't sure you'd want your name on her writing."

"It's her name, too!"

"I think if she gets back with you, she'll want to go by Denise Donnelly hyphen Westfield."

Jerry grimaced. "Hell! What's this world coming to?"

"Smile. I hear her coming."

Denise had lost weight and wore a chic minidress, bursting with yellow Pop Art flowers. She'd cut her hair into a shoulder-length pageboy with long, sexy bangs that dipped over her dark, smoldering eyes. Jerry looked at her so long, I thought he was going to drool on his shirt.

Denise noticed me and her eyes narrowed. "What's going on?" She looked into the living room as if she expected to find our whole family there, waiting to ambush her in some sort of intervention.

"I'm here to chaperone," I said cheerfully. Actually it was to referee.

She sniffed. "And you cooked dinner?"

"Nope. Jerry did."

"Jerry can't boil water."

"That was lesson one," he said. "Joanne taught me. I can't guarantee how good the meat loaf will be. This is my first try. Have a seat."

Jerry pulled out a chair for Denise, thought better of it, then pushed it back so that she nearly landed on the floor. Denise and I seated ourselves, and Jerry served us before taking his place.

"Everything looks beautiful," said Denise.

"Thanks." Jerry took a bite of meat loaf and began looking around the table.

"Oh, the salt," said Denise, starting to rise. "I'll get it."

*"Harrumph! Harrumph!"* I cleared my throat loudly, and Denise sat back down.

Denise looked at Jerry, and Jerry looked at Denise. I think it hurt them both a little that Jerry got up to get the salt, when Denise had gotten it for him dozens of times in their short marriage.

"Does your aunt come in to do the apartment?" asked Denise.

"Joanne is my slave."

"Oh, I am not! Jerry cleans the apartment himself."

"Yep, yep," said Jerry. "It's all true. I cook, clean. Just your regular little houseboy, I am."

I jabbed him with a flying elbow.

"Ow!"

Denise giggled.

Jerry took her hand. "You look really pretty."

"Pretty?" I exclaimed. "Knockout gorgeous."

Denise smiled back at Jerry. "You look pretty good yourself, but you've got a little scorch under your arm."

Jerry checked his sleeve under his armpit. "Damn! Ironing isn't easy."

When the main course was finished, I rose to help Jerry clear the table. "I got it, Beethoven. Just relax. Ice cream is coming up."

"Certainly I can help our gracious host clear."

"Let him do it, Joanne. I'm enjoying this." Denise gazed up at Jerry, who leered down at her. Who needed ice cream? They looked ready to have each other for dessert.

I was trying to think of a graceful exit when Denise asked, "How's your dissertation going, Jerry?"

"A little slower now that I'm working at the copy shop, but it's going." He set dishes of ice cream before us and sat down.

"I wish it weren't on Freud," said Denise. "He's done so much harm to women."

"Not true. He was a great comfort to many women suffering from hysteria. Through psychoanalysis he was able to alleviate their symptoms of hallucinations, amnesia, and paralysis."

Denise's prim mouth tightened. "This so-called hysteria in women was brought about because in Freud's time women were prohibited from doing important work."

"They could do important work. They just didn't have any."

Denise let her spoon drop with a clatter. "Freud thought the female sex was an incurable disease!"

Jerry paused and looked under the table. "Just checking to see if you still shave your legs."

"I *still* shave my legs! And you're *still* a chauvinist pig!" Denise grabbed her purse and stalked out of the apartment, slamming the door so hard the salt shaker fell over.

"That went well," said Jerry.

I raised a forefinger. "Up to a point."

# CHAPTER
# NINETEEN

At sunrise, tambourines and drums echoed through Buena Vista Park, where Martin and I stood with about a hundred other people. It was October 6, three days after my seventeenth birthday, and we were participating in another hippie celebration, "Birth of the Free Spirit." Like other "Happenings" in Haight-Ashbury, it was street theater, partly serious, partly burlesque. The important thing seemed to be that individuals were a part of something bigger than themselves, many people becoming one, the same kind of feeling you got on LSD, illegal now for two years.

We lit candles and began to process down Haight Street, which was decorated with banners reading BIRTH OF THE FREE SPIRIT.

Martin raised his fist in the air and shouted, "Be free! Be free! Be free!"

I felt shackled. Only a month of my senior year had passed, and it felt like an eternity until I graduated. "The crowd is pretty thin," I said. "Not like last year."

He waved his hand. "But look at all these impostors still hanging on. The real hippies got crowded out by all the plastic ones. It's time to just be people again. Real people. Individuals."

At the intersection of Haight and Ashbury, I looked up at the street sign and marveled at such a landmark being so close to my own home. The procession continued into Golden Gate Park and onto Hippie Hill, people chanting, "Be free! Be free!" Some people yanked off their hats, bandanas, love beads, and other articles of clothing and flung them into the trees.

Martin threw his beads, and they caught on a high branch. "Now yours," he said to me.

I tucked mine under my shirt. "I could never part with these beads. They're the first thing you ever gave me."

"Celebrate, Joni! The Age of Aquarius is over. It was all just a dream, a lovely dream."

"Say it was more than that, Martin."

"Peace and love and brotherhood? We can still hope for these things, but everything comes to an end." Martin looked down at the ground and then back up at me. "There's something else that has to end, Joni. Byron quit Roach, and Bread is pretty much useless. They'll never cut that album. They're a one-hit wonder. Gus still doesn't see it. He can't let go. He wants me to join the band, and you know how I feel about that. It's best I move on."

My heart was beating fast. "What do you mean 'move on'?" I asked cautiously.

"There are some people I know who have a house in Sacramento who will let me stay with them."

My vision blurred with my tears. What about me? I wanted to scream at him. What about us? I knew we'd have to part someday, but I was not expecting it to be so soon or so sudden.

"Hey, this isn't good-bye, Joni. I'll still come down to the city to see you, and you can come see me."

He reached for me, but I crossed my arms and twisted away. I looked up into the tree where his beads hung, far out of my reach. I knew how it would be. Martin would promise to come visit me, stick out his thumb, and end up someplace completely different. Whole weeks and months would go by in Martin time while I sat waiting, waiting, waiting.

"You're wrong, Martin. It is good-bye." I faced him and stuck out my hand to shake. "So long. It's been nice knowing you."

"Joni, Joni, don't be that way." He scooped me up in his arms and somehow my arms went around him. I sobbed and sobbed and wondered how I could ever let him go.

I looked into those beautiful eyes of my beautiful hippie, and even as angry as I was with him, I wanted one last kiss. It was sad and sweet, long and loving, and then I broke away and ran down Hippie Hill, across Stanyan, and up Frederick Street.

I didn't stop until I reached my very own pink bedroom. I had intended to throw myself on the bed and cry some more, but Mom had set a letter on my desk. It was in a thin, pale blue *par avion* envelope used for overseas mail, but it wasn't from Jimmy. I tore it open. Its author introduced himself as Jimmy's sergeant. He said he knew I was Jimmy's girl; Jimmy had talked about me all the time. The sergeant felt this letter would be a kinder, gentler way of letting me know. The news was hard enough for me to take. It would be harder for Dan.

I found him in the den watching TV. I shut off the set, and when he opened his mouth to protest, he looked at me and didn't speak.

I sat next to him on the sofa. My tears for Martin's leaving and Jimmy's dying were all mixed up and flowing down my face. "I'm sorry, Dan. I have bad news. It's Jimmy Howe. He...didn't make it."

"That can't be right! Where'd you hear that?"

I set the letter on his knee. "At your New Year's Eve party, Jimmy asked me to write him, just as a pen pal, you know, and well...this one is from his sergeant."

Dan looked down at the letter a long moment. "I don't want the fucking thing! Get it off me!" He slapped the envelope, and it fluttered to the carpet.

# CHAPTER
## TWENTY

At first I couldn't believe Martin was really gone. He'll miss me, I thought. He loves me too much to leave me. I moved like a zombie from school to home to piano lessons and master classes to home again, going through the motions of living, waiting for Martin to come back. It amazed me, actually, how much I hurt. Wasn't I an independent girl, leading a rich, full life? How could Martin's leaving matter so much? Love happens. It's hard to understand what all it can do to a person.

At school, Rena had eased into Lisa's place in the in crowd, yukking it up with Candy Lambert. Rena and I were friendly, but the closeness we'd once shared had evaporated. Isn't that the way with friendships? One person is your best friend one year, and then it's someone else the next. But I'd thought Rena and I would be for always, even when we were old ladies. Some days I looked across the school yard expecting to see Suyu in her usual spot, waving her arms, caught up in her imaginary practice. I thought of her far away at MIT and hoped she was happy working with her computers.

One day I opened the Ravel *"Sonatine"* Dr. Harold had given me nearly a year ago. I'd done nothing but picked at it on occasion, never taking it in for a lesson. Now I began to practice it in earnest. Is it possible to live inside a piece of music? I could say I lived in the Ravel. That piece was my consolation, my shelter, my purpose. Still, there were times when I couldn't concentrate at the piano. I caught myself playing more and more softly so I could hear my thoughts, and sometimes my hands slipped off the keys and I was just sitting there, staring vacantly at the music but seeing Martin's face.

One afternoon, I was startled to find my mother beside me on the piano bench as if we were about to launch into "Heart and Soul."

"Did you and Martin break up?"

"We were never going steady."

"Did you stop dating?"

"We never went on dates."

"I don't see him coming around anymore."

"He moved away, Mom."

She patted my shoulder, which made me cry. "You'll have other boyfriends, Joanne."

"Oh, Mom, it hurts. I never thought anything would hurt this much."

"I know, honey." She kissed my hair. "Give it some time."

She didn't tell me to stop moping, and she didn't say what a lazy good-for-nothing Martin was. I was impressed by how sympathetic she was. Later that afternoon, though, I overheard her on the telephone gloating to Thelma, "The hippie's gone. Good riddance! Joanne is pretty broken up about it, but she'll snap out of it."

I wished I could snap out of it. My problems seemed so much smaller than everyone else's. Denise and Jerry were still separated. In November Nixon was elected president. Another Dick. It seemed the Vietnam War would rage on. Dan stopped doing push-ups. He stopped going out drinking with his buddies. He stopped saying much at all. Sometimes late at night I heard Mom helping him change his sheets. He had night sweats that soaked his entire bed.

I forced myself to get out more. I roamed the neighborhood, which was much quieter. By then the Free Clinic had closed its doors, and so had the Matrix and the Trip Without a Ticket. In all, I counted eighteen vacant storefronts on Haight. Love Burgers was still around, and so were Tracy's Donuts and the Psyche Shop. I tried not to superimpose Martin on all our favorite haunts.

One afternoon after school while drinking tea in the Tangerine Kangaroo, I got to playing the Ravel in my mind, as I often did. I came to a part I wasn't sure of, and it annoyed me that I couldn't think what came next. I eyed the piano sitting alone in the corner. I went up to it and started playing Ravel. Over the past year, something had happened inside me, so that a slip of the finger or the sound of a shutting door no longer bothered my performance. I just didn't care anymore that I wasn't perfect, and that changed my playing. Being an accomplished pianist was no longer a destination, but a process. Each time I sat down at the piano I tried to make music, and sometimes I would be satisfied with my efforts, while other times I would be discouraged, but that's just the way it is with anything worth doing.

I reached the section of the Ravel that I was wondering about, and having played what came before it, I had no trouble continuing. When I finished the movement, I was startled to hear applause. I turned around and bowed. Practicing in public, I suppose, was a kind of performing.

One stormy night while I was home alone practicing, I thought I heard a knock on the back door. I paused, listening, and then decided it was only the wind. A few minutes later the doorbell startled me.

I turned on the foyer light, looked through the peephole in the front door, and saw Pete Wattle, soaking wet.

I opened the door to say, "Dan's not here."

"Can I come in a minute?" Pete asked, wiping his feet on the mat.

I reluctantly opened the door wider to let him pass, irritated that he'd interrupted me. "Dan is working the late shift. I can tell him you stopped by."

"What's going on with you?"

"Me? I'm just playing the piano."

"Can I listen awhile?"

"I guess. It's just practicing, though."

Pete sat on the sofa, and I went back to hammering out the four measures I'd been working on. The sound of his breathing was annoying. I couldn't concentrate with someone else in the room. I wished he'd leave.

"Why do you play the piano so much?" he blurted.

I stopped to glare at him. "Because I hate it."

"Okay, dumb question."

"Dan will probably be real late. There's no use hanging around waiting for him."

"I know." He looked around the room but didn't rise from the sofa. "Hey, Joanne, Simon and Garfunkel are coming to the Masonic Auditorium. Wanna go?"

"How much?"

"You wouldn't have to pay."

"Why not?" He didn't answer, color seeping into his face. It took me a few seconds to realize he was asking me out on a date. "Oh." I didn't know what else to say.

"Forget it." He got up and let himself out the front door.

I listened to his footsteps and heard the front gate clank before darting to the door, flinging it open, and shouting against the wind. "Yes! I want to go! Thanks, Pete. They're my favorite."

"I know," he hollered back.

I was surprised at how nervous I was, waiting for Pete to pick me up. It was, after all, my first official date. I was wearing my denim bell-bottoms and tie-dye T-shirt. Dad took one look at me and said, "No daughter of mine is wearing pants to the Masonic Auditorium. Go change, Joanne."

I stomped up to my room and changed into a dress and heels. Pete's eyes popped when I answered the door. He was wearing a suit and tie, so I was glad I'd gotten dressed up, too.

At his car, he unlocked the passenger-side door and paused. "Do you want me to open the door for you?"

I shrugged. "Why not?"

"A guy has to be careful these days. Some girls think it's being polite, other girls have a cow."

After we parked, I got out while Pete ran around the car to the passenger's side. He seemed disappointed to see me standing on the curb waiting for him. "I thought you liked me to open the car door for you."

"When you unlock it, you might as well open it, but I'm not going to sit around waiting."

Pete pretended to remove a notepad from his jacket pocket. "Likes to have the door opened for her getting into the car—check. Does not like the door opened getting out of the car—check."

He made me laugh, and that felt good.

At the concert, the audience was quieter than usual. At times we could even hear the music. While Simon and Garfunkel sang "Sounds of Silence," Pete took my hand.

Afterward we went for late-night sandwiches at the Tangerine Kangaroo. It was strange to be sitting there all dressed up, with someone other than Martin.

"I know Dan is freaked out about getting drafted," said Pete. "I feel for the guy. I'm hanging on to my student deferment as long as I can. I don't want to kill anybody."

Martin had once said those same words to me, and I liked hearing them coming from Pete. He could merely have said he didn't want to die.

When I asked him what he was studying, he said, "Computers."

"I know somebody who studies computers at MIT."

"Wow! He must be a genius to get in there."

"She."

"Wow," he said, shaking his head. "Far out."

On our porch, I thanked Pete for a lovely evening.

"I think you're cool, Joanne," he said, and then he kissed me soft and quick.

Nothing stirred in me like when Martin kissed me, but I figured that was okay.

Pete kept asking me on dates, and I kept accepting. We didn't have much in common. He took me to car shows that didn't interest me, and I took him to classical music concerts that made him fidget. We both liked going to the movies. In his arms I could heal from the loss of Martin, take a rest, knowing I could never fall in love with him. He was comforting and safe. He never came on hot and heavy. He was a lot of laughs. Sometimes we included Dan in our plans, which seemed to pull him out of his self-pity.

One day I was walking home from school, smiling to myself about something Pete had said. Rena caught up with me and bumped my shoulder. "Hey, you. I've been yelling for a block trying to get your attention. You look happy. Are you in love?"

"No, but I'm in like." I realized I was doing better, and a lot of it was because of Pete. I confided in Rena about how I felt dating Pete, and it was almost like old times between us.

I dropped her off at Walker Street and hiked on up the hill to my house. I opened the mailbox, and there was the postcard. It had the white dome of the capitol building on it and a big, fat camellia in front of that. It said WELCOME TO SACRAMENTO.

Martin's message was brief: "Hey, Joni, I love you! I miss you! Come visit! Next Saturday would be cool. Don't know how much longer I'll be around." Below were his address, a peace sign, and his signature.

Damn! Damn! Damn you, Martin!

I was almost past him, nearly back to normal, and now this! Hope welled up within me like a poisonous weed. Here was Martin, wanting to see me, and how could I refuse him?

I ran all the way back to Rena's and showed her the postcard. "I want to go see him, but I don't want to be hurt again. What do I do?"

"Resist, Joanne, resist. Why try to start something up again when it will only give you grief?"

"I know, but—"

"But what? I don't know what you saw in him in the first place. I mean, it was cool he's the brother of Gus Abbott and all that, but Roach is broken up now."

"That wasn't why I loved Martin."

Rena was shaking her head. "He's bad news. Here, let me make it easy for you." She snatched my wonderful postcard, and before I could stop her, she tore it into pieces and handed it back to me. "There you go," she said with a smug smile, and in that instant I hated her.

# CHAPTER
## TWENTY-ONE

On the cold December morning when Dan was scheduled to make the train trip from Oakland to Fort Riley, Kansas, for U. S. Army boot camp, he had talked our family into saying our good-byes at home.

"I don't want you embarrassing me at the train station, crying and stuff," he said. "It's going to be hard enough."

The previous day Denise had taken Dan out to lunch, Jerry had met him for a beer, and Pete and I had thrown him a small party with a few of their old high school friends. Now it was just Mom, Dad, and me, standing on the curb in front of our house seeing him off. Dad shook his hand, Mom kissed him, and I hugged him. Dan muttered his good-byes, but he wouldn't look into our faces. I supposed he didn't want to cry. We watched him shoulder his back pack, cross the street, and head down Masonic to catch the streetcar.

It was all so anticlimactic. Just like any other Thursday morning, Dad drove off to work, Thelma picked up Mom to go to their garden club project, and I started my walk to school.

But I didn't want to go to school. I dreaded seeing Rena and Candy and those guys. My classes were boring and so was Pete, and I was sick of practicing Ravel. With me being the only kid at home, Mom would spend all her energy picking on me.

I made it as far up Haight as the east side of Buena Vista

Park. I circled back and headed home. In my room, I went to my desk and took out all my savings and the tattered shreds of Martin's postcard. I fitted them together like the pieces of a jigsaw puzzle or a broken heart. I had already memorized the address, and on a map of Sacramento I'd found in our map drawer, I'd penciled in a route from the train station to Martin.

I packed my music satchel with my toothbrush, hairbrush, and change of clothes. In the kitchen, I thought to leave a note under the salt shaker, but it seemed too sad, like the song "She's Leaving Home" on the *Sgt. Pepper* album. I wouldn't be as cruel as Lisa Girardi and disappear without a trace; I'd call my parents in a few days. None of this was planned. I was amazed by my own behavior, as if I were a bystander watching someone else live my life.

Traveling by streetcar, bus, train, bus again, and finally my own feet, it took me until four o'clock to get to Martin's. I found him lounging on a front porch swing, reading Steinbeck's *Travels with Charley.* He sprang up to greet me.

"Whoa, Joni! What a surprise! Why aren't you in school today?"

"I ditched."

He gave me a kiss. It wasn't passionate, but rather like a cool glass of water I'd been thirsting for. "I think I've been thinking about you so much I willed you here. Come on in and meet everybody."

We went into the house and sat around talking to a bunch of his housemates I didn't care about. Together we fixed dinner and ate. The whole time I was thinking I just wanted to be alone with Martin, to hold him in my arms, to kiss him and kiss him.

Finally he led me to a bedroom with bare walls and clean surfaces. In a corner were a huge backpack and a bedroll, neatly packed. "You nearly missed me, Joni. I'm headed out tomorrow."

"Where to?"

He shrugged. "To wherever my thumb takes me. I'm off on my great American adventure."

"Where's your guitar?"

"Pawned it to buy this stuff. Pretty neat setup, huh?"

"Martin, I didn't come here just for a visit. I want to stay with you."

He actually laughed. "I don't think your piano will fit in a backpack."

"I don't care about that."

"Yes, you do. You *want* to want to live like me, but in fact you don't. You need to get home, Joni, finish high school, go to college, and play those recitals in Carnegie Hall."

"I'm not good enough for Carnegie Hall."

"You don't know that. It's too soon to tell. Anyway, Carnegie Hall is beside the point. You'll play those recitals somewhere."

"How do you know?"

"It's who you are. You won't be able to stop yourself."

I held him tight and buried my face in his chest. "I have to be with you, Martin. You're the only one who understands me. I've tried to live without you, but you've left this big, empty void in my life that I can't fill. Can't you come back to San Francisco? Can't we find a way to be together?"

He pressed his forehead against mine. I saw that he was crying, too. "We want different things," he whispered. "Couldn't you see that from the beginning?"

I didn't want to see it, not even now. "I can't let you go!"

"We've got tonight."

We fell on the bed and caressed and kissed for a very long time. Finally, he whispered, "Let's make love."

I turned my face to the wall and felt my tears drip off the side of my nose onto the pillow. I didn't know much about sex, but I did know that making love was the beginning of a relationship, not the end of one. Martin cuddled against me and massaged little circles in my back until his hand went still and he began to breathe deeply. I told myself, Leave, you've got to leave. There's no place for you here. I thought about my parents back at home, calling the school, finding out I hadn't gone today, thinking of Lisa Girardi, and worrying about me.

Martin was right, of course. My place was home with Mom

and Dad. They were the ones who loved me, who would never abandon me. My life was that of a regular middle-class teenage girl, who just happened to have lived in Haight-Ashbury during the Summer of Love.

When I got up, the springs of the bed creaked. Martin rolled into the hollow of the worn mattress. I stared at his calm, moon-lit face, but I didn't touch him. Good-bye, my beautiful hippie, I thought, and then I crept out of the house.

I cried nearly the whole train ride back to Emeryville. Not with audible sobs, but merely with tears trickling down my face. I thought I heard a rending sound. It was my mind letting Martin go, or trying to. Yearnings such as I had do not die sudden deaths. This could take years. I thought how chemotherapy sometimes kills the body before it can kill the cancer, but no one ever dies of a broken heart, not without the help of a gun.

It was nearly one a.m. when the Amtrak bus pulled into the Ferry Building Station. Public transit had stopped running at midnight, and I had no doubt worried my parents long enough. I used nearly all my savings to take a taxi from the Embarcadero to my house. I would tell Mom and Dad the truth for once. I would try to be a better daughter. They were good parents, and if they'd hurt me or made some mistakes, they had merely done the best they could.

I paid the cabdriver and let myself in the gate. On our small lawn was a yellow square of light shooting out from the kitchen, where my parents were probably waiting up for me.

They weren't there. In fact, the house was empty. Under-neath the salt shaker was a note from Mom. "Joanne, fix your-self some dinner if we don't get home in time. Dad and I have gone looking for Dan. Love, Mom."

Wasn't Dan...? Hadn't Dan...? He hadn't been able to look into our faces, and now I knew why.

Awhile later my parents shuffled through the back door. They moved slowly, in a state of shock. Mom sank into a kitchen chair, gazing vacantly before her, while Dad put the coffee on to perk.

"Joanne, did you know Denise left Jerry?" asked Mom.

"Yes," I replied softly.

She went on as if she hadn't heard me. "Their apartment was one of the places we looked for Dan. Jerry was there alone. He admitted he and Denise haven't been living together since the beginning of summer. I just don't understand. Why are all my children running away? You're the flighty one, Joanne."

"I'm not going anywhere, Mom."

Dad told me how he had lied to the United States government. When Dan didn't show in time to board his train out of Oakland, his recruiting officer called our house, asking where he was. Dad told him we had gotten our dates confused, that Dan was off saying good-bye to relatives. He promised that Dan would be on the next train out of Oakland the following day.

"This happens sometimes," the recruiting officer had said. "Just have him here tomorrow and everything will be okay."

First we had to find him. If the government found him first, he would probably have to go to jail for going AWOL.

Dad had just poured the coffee when Jerry and Denise came through the back door. They told us about all the phone calls they had made and all the places they had looked for Dan.

The phone rang. Mom started. Dad looked toward the hall. It rang again. "I'll get it," he said.

"Listen, son," we heard Dad say into the telephone, "everything's all right. I talked to your recruiting officer, and he said you can ship out tomorrow. He understands about cold feet. You're not in trouble with the law, not yet. There's still time to set things right.... No, son, we're not mad. Maybe a little disappointed... Straighten up, Dan! Be a man! Now, listen, I'm going to wire you some money. Make sure you're on the next flight to San Francisco."

Dad returned to the kitchen. "He's okay! He's coming home. He just lost his nerve is all. He took the Greyhound bus to Vancouver, Washington, and was about to cross over to Vancouver, Canada, when he lost his nerve again."

"We raised him right," said Mom. "He has a conscience."

"Let's hope so," said Dad. He returned to the phone to dial Western Union.

The big question was in all our minds, although no one spoke it: Would Dan use the money Dad wired him to fly home, or would he use it to start a new life in Canada?

# CHAPTER
# TWENTY-TWO

Dad took off work, and I didn't go to school. My parents, Denise, Jerry, and I all got into the Oldsmobile with Dan to see him off at the Oakland train station. Nobody said much on the drive across the bay. We were all bleary-eyed from staying up most of the night. Dan's flight from Vancouver had gotten into San Francisco at eight a.m., and Dad had gone over to the airport to pick him up. Now we were running late for Dan's ten o'clock train departure to Fort Riley. We had to park several blocks away because hundreds of other families had already arrived to drop their boys off.

We stood around with only a few minutes to spare before Dan had to board the train. Denise and Jerry were holding hands. In the early hours of the morning, Denise had told Jerry she was returning to Cal as an English major in January, and Jerry had told Denise that he had redirected his dissertation to "Making Meaning of Psychoanalysis through the Women's Movement." With my parents' help, they had talked things out and had decided to get back together.

Now I could see that Mom was trying hard not to cry. Dad delivered his pep talk to Dan in a steady, strong voice. "We're proud of you, son. You're doing the right thing. When Uncle Sam calls you up, you've got to serve, no questions asked. You'll come out of this thing okay, God willing."

I stared hard at my brother, burning his face into my memory, thinking of Jimmy Howe disappearing into the darkness at the top of our stairs.

It was time. We gave Dan last-minute hugs, and then he boarded the train. We thought that was the last we'd see of him, but then his face appeared at an upper-deck window. He spotted us and broke into a wide, forlorn grin. I waved so furiously it felt like my hand might fly off my wrist. Dan looked right at me and splayed two fingers. Peace.

Jerry and Denise had to catch a bus to Berkeley, but my parents and I waited to watch the train roll out of sight. Then we walked toward Dad's Oldsmobile.

"It's just the three of us now," said Mom. "What are you going to do with yourself, Joanne?"

I shrugged. "The usual stuff."

"Well, do you have a date with Pete tonight?"

"Naw." After being with Martin one last time, dating Pete felt like a lie. "I've decided he's not my type."

"And I suppose Martin was."

"Nope. He wasn't, either."

"Who is your type?" she asked.

"Beethoven!"

"Oh, he had a normal life with the wife and kids!" Dad chimed in.

"You know what I mean." As soon as I got home, I was going to pull out my Beethoven sonata and blow off the dust. I knew quite a bit more about myself and the world than the last time I had played it, and I would have a whole new interpretation.

"You should take up typing," Dad said, not seriously, but in a gently teasing way.

"Daddy, I know how to type! I'm more practical than you think. If I have to type, I will type, but nothing boring and stupid like Mr. Marlowe's letters. It will have to be something important."

"Like what?" asked Mom.

Something that would change the world, but of course I couldn't tell my parents that; they'd only laugh at me. Mrs. Scudder, who was getting on in years, had invited me into her studio to teach the beginners, so I had a job that wasn't typing. By now I knew I wasn't going to Juilliard; I was pretty certain my parents would get their wish to see one of their kids graduate from San Francisco State, but I was planning on moving out as soon as I could.

I swung my arms around both my parents. In the past year, I had grown a couple of inches taller than my mom, so I had to lean over to kiss her forehead.

"What was that for?" she asked.

I didn't answer. She knew.